*I think we should
go into the jungle*

I think we should
go into the jungle

short stories by

BARBARA ANDERSON

Victoria University Press

VICTORIA UNIVERSITY PRESS
Victoria University of Wellington
PO Box 600 Wellington

© Barbara Anderson 1989

ISBN 0 86473 079 9

Published with the assistance of a grant from the
Literary Fund of the Queen Elizabeth II Arts Council

National Library of New Zealand
Cataloguing-in-Publication data

Anderson, Barbara, 1926–
    I think we should go into the jungle : short
stories / by Barbara Anderson. Wellington [N.Z.] :
Victoria University Press, c1989.
    1 v.
    Short stories.
    ISBN 0864730799 (pbk.)
I. Title.
    NZ823.2

ACKNOWLEDGEMENTS

Some of these stories have been previously published in
Landfall, the Listener, Sport, Metro and the Timaru Herald
or broadcast by Radio New Zealand

The author gratefully acknowledges the assistance of a
project grant from the Literary Fund of the Queen
Elizabeth II Arts Council during the
completion of this book.

Typeset by Saba Graphics Ltd, Christchurch
Printed in Hong Kong through Bookprint
Consultants Ltd, Wellington.

Contents

For Neil

Discontinuous Lives

I am pouring the tea at my cousin's house after her funeral and there are many special requests. — No milk please, just a dash, is there a stronger one, where's the sugar. But that is how it is wherever I am pouring so why not at a funeral. We have brought extra cups. There are green ones with primroses, wine coloured ones with gold rims and Andrea's blue and white. Most people have one by now, the women that is, the men have whisky. Amber curls in each glass for comfort for that is how it is at funerals, though maybe a sherry later for some of the girls. Another cousin, Maureen, says into my ear as I turn my head checking for cupless female hands — That's Morris Baker.

— Morris who? I say, then remember. — Morris Baker! Where?

— Over there, Maureen points.

— But it's a woman!

— Didn't you know? A pseudonym.

— No! Goodness me, how extraordinary, and I have to regroup, my cousin's silver-plated teapot left hanging because I am so surprised, like when I found Auden's 'Lay your sleeping head my love' was written to a man, to say nothing of Shakespeare's sonnets. Why not, and many men

BARBARA ANDERSON

have most beautiful hair but it is a different head I see
laid human on that faithless arm, and now Morris Baker.

Morris Baker is a large woman, deep bosomed. It finishes
not far above her belt having swelled out at the usual place.
She wears an expensive easy-care which has small purple
and black checks. Her dark grey hair is swept back from
her strong features and her expression is serene and what
on earth is this world famous novelist (albeit of yesteryear)
doing at Diane's funeral on Bluff Hill, I gasp.

— Didn't you know? says Maureen again. — She was
born in the Bay, at Clive.

— No indeed. Fancy that. Fancy *A Man in Grey, A Nettle
Grasped, Whither Stranger* and all the rest of them coming from
Clive, for heaven's sake!

— No no no, says Maureen rescuing the teapot which
has begun to dribble onto Diane's brown carpet of which
she was so proud. — They left years ago, went back to
England, her parents were English, they got fed up. It must
have been after you left. I can remember when she went.
What a party, she was a beautiful girl.

— And still is. How amazing, I must meet her. Why is
she out?

— There's a brother or something. She lives in Burford
now, you know in England.

But this cannot be. I lived in Burford for years and if
anyone came from New Zealand, let alone a famous novelist
(I was there in yesteryear) I would have met her because
everyone would have said — There is another New
Zealander living in Burford you must meet her.

Whether you want to or not.

— Perhaps it had an E or something, says Maureen.

— Yes perhaps, though I am puzzled.

By now people are coming back for second cups and I
am pouring again and reboiling the kettle and Morris Baker
has to keep.

We stack the cups on the steel bench, looking out over

the grapefruit tree which did well for us all because Diane was generous. — We'll do them later we say, nodding wisely at the cups and saucers and each other. We know what to do. I wipe my hands on a tea towel I sent Diane from Burford which has a picture of Anne Hathaway's cottage on it and move back to the front room which is crowded with my cousin's friends and relations. A neighbour shows me the spot where he found my cousin. — It was *there*, he says pointing. — There. I stare at the carpet beneath his craggy finger and nod. — Yes, I say. Yes.

There is quite a lot of noise by now. — Diane would be pleased we say, but do we know. We know she liked people and parties. — Where would I be without my friends she would ask as we arrived with another jar of soup to stuff in her refrigerator and always on New Year's Eve she let her hair down but we still don't know. Like when middle-aged children say at a parent's demise, Mother would hate to have been a nuisance. Have they seen it in writing.

Morris Baker is by the window, the neighbour is pointing at the carpet, Morris Baker is nodding. I move over quickly, my hand outstretched. — Hullo, I'm Elaine Wilkinson, I just want to say I've always loved your books. Morris Baker is pleased. She puts down her empty cup which we must have missed and holds out her hand. I remember from Burford about women shaking hands, it does not happen in Napier so much though occasionally, prize-givings for example. Her hand is warm and soft, the bones beneath are strong. If Morris Baker shakes hands like this in Burford the ladies must be surprised and I bet she does. She smiles at me, a beautiful warm wide embracing smile. Her eyes are large and brown and I am delighted to meet her and this shows as we beam at each other holding hands.

— Which book did you like best? asks Morris Baker.
— *Whither Stranger*, I say. — Yes that is my favourite, she replies.
— Tell me what you meant at the end did Rupert . . .

Morris Baker flings back her smooth coiled head to laugh deeply. — Ah no, she says, you mustn't ask me that, how do I know.

There is too much noise.

— Come into the spare room, I say, so we move to the door into the hall, touching people gently to show respect for my cousin Diane who is dead.

The hall is narrow and empty, there are coats on the hooks and a beater which someone brought for the cream but didn't need lies on the carpet. The telephone my cousin loved sits round-shouldered and silent, grieving on its table.

My cousin was not a believer. She was bonny and blithe and good and gay and saved me when I returned from Burford in despair, having tried matrimony and failed.

Morris Baker and I have reached the spare room. It is very simple. Every penny my cousin Diane had she earned in the library, unqualified and cheerful. There are two single beds covered in glazed chintz 'all over' pattern of pink rosebuds and blue ribbons which loop and scroll to encircle each bud. She made these on her ancient Singer inherited from Auntie Dot when the more affluent were converting them into wrought-iron Outdoor Tables. She frilled the valances and attached them firmly so that the crass hot pink of the sprung base was hidden. She ran up the curtains. All this I know and ignore as Morris Baker and I sit one on each bed knee to knee though mine are higher and we continue our in depth discussion of Morris Baker's books.

— I always thought that you left the ending of *Whither Stranger* so *unresolved*, I say.

— Well of course.

— Yes I know. I mean I know you meant to but . . .

Morris Baker laughs an in depth gurgle of pleasure. She stabs a hand down the front of her dress and produces a small white handkerchief. I am not to be put off.

— I know you meant to I say, leaning forward with my hands on my knees, but I still think . . . I mean we don't even know if Rupert *stays*.

Morris Baker dabs at the end of her dry nose with her handkerchief.

— I have left you, that is the reader, she says, imaginative space.

— Yes I know and I like that, I say, — but don't you think that in this case you might have just . . . The unspoken word 'cheated' stains the silence. I have gone too far. I am now an anxious placating figure, a shadow of that switched on bibliophile whose behind creased the roses opposite Morris Baker's.

But Morris Baker is an old pro, a trouper, she takes the rough with the smooth, she wins some she loses some, she rides with the punches, she takes it on the chin and comes back fighting.

— How can you, she says smiling with large white teeth (I envy to gut bitterness those with the white sort) — How can you say in the same breath that you like imaginative space and yet you feel I've cheated by leaving you, the reader, just that.

— Goodness me! I gasp. I didn't say that.

— No you didn't say it, says Morris Baker, but I heard it.

This is better than ever. Morris Baker is an opponent worthy of the steel of one who has slogged through extramural English and a hard time we had of it I'm here to tell you.

— What I meant was, I say laughing with my yellow teeth for amiability, what I meant was that I think there is a difference between the author leaving the reader imaginative space and just not knowing . . . Again the words melt and fizzle. The cut and thrust of literary criticism is one thing, a tea pourer being rude to a famous author at her friend's funeral is another. How can I say '. . . not knowing how to finish'.

— Not knowing how to finish, says Morris Baker.

I toss my head to show how merry my laugh is. The curls bounce in the three-sided mirror attached to the

11

dressing table. I look away quickly and focus instead on three mats embroidered by my late cousin which lie upon its horizontal surface. The larger one lies in the middle, a smaller supporter graces each side. Embroidered upon each is a lady in a crinoline. Three faces are hidden by poke bonnets, three flesh-pink mini hands hold parasols, six tiny feet wade among buttonhole stitch forget-me-nots, lazy daisies, and blades of single stitch grass. The two smaller mats have proportionally smaller ladies but the blossoms of their flowering fields are the same size. Each mat is edged with crochet in a colour called ecru. As a diversion from Morris Baker's acuteness I heave myself up from the bed and hold up the large mat.

— Diane made these, I say.

— Good Lord, laughs Morris Baker.

This comment has the small shock of a cobweb in the face. It clings. It won't do. I brush it away.

— Tell me about your life, I babble. When did you leave the Bay? What was your real name?

— Beryl Hollings, she says.

The years slough off, a crumpled discard. — Beryl, Beryl, I scream, seizing her hands. — I'm Elaine Nimmo! We are hugging and laughing and laughing and, No, Go on, Of course, Of course, I knew I knew you, we lie, but not quite, I did have a feeling. We laugh some more, touching for warmth, touching for contact, touching for old times and remembering and for the wonder of our lives and reunion after so long when we had almost forgotten we existed, the other one that is.

They were different the Hollings, being English for a start.

And they weren't at Clive as Maureen said, just Greenmeadows like we were, but too far to bike so Beryl and I played together on parent-arranged visits, the worst sort.

— Aw hang Mum do I have to go, it smells. It is not the smell which worries me but I don't know how to express unease, and hope to touch a sympathetic chord. My mother dislikes smells. — It *whats?* — Smells. — Nonsense! My mother lifts her head momentarily from her bedmaking demonstration. Her hands continue their origami-like pleating and tucking of the blankets; she insists on hospital corners. — What a fuss pot, she laughs. I spot the contradiction, but though hospital corners may defeat me I know about answering back.

The Hollings house did smell; a close, layered smell, airless and nicotined. The French doors never opened onto the wide verandah except for the huffing exit of Dinky the canker-eared spaniel.

They had brought their things with them from Home and crammed them into the small square rooms. The Drawing Room was the worst. A mahogany bureau faded beside a brass-bound sea chest (male) and a small davenport (female). Occasional tables teetered at a touch. There was no room to move. — No space, no space, moaned Mrs Hollings, drifting and dreaming of height and width, of gentler suns and softer airs. She cut up cucumbers and 'applied' them to her pale skin. She did what she could.

Captain Hollings was a small explosive man described by my Uncle Bob as a no hoper and thus watched with interest as he stumped about clutching a stick for support. He had lost a leg in the war. Where? How?

The Captain rose late. His pretend leg, its attachment end slack-jawed and empty, waited beside his disordered bed as he made a good breakfast and Beryl and Mrs Hollings scurried in and out with replacements in response to his roars. — Marmalade! — Toast! Dinky lay at his feet, a golden lump beneath the eiderdown, buried deep in his foetid smell.

After several false starts Beryl and I became friends. My father and I swept up the drive in the Buick, hammered the bored lion's head knocker against the door till Mrs Hollings, distracted and unnerved by any summons, yanked the door open, her fingers fluttering against her mouth for protection. She apologised for everything, anything, the stuck door, her apron, the lack of decent rain for the farmers,

13

her very existence. She made me want to cry. My father waited hat in hand and departed as soon as possible. Beryl appeared behind her mother and stuck her tongue out at me in greeting. Her mother's hunted glance fell on us. — Well now chicks what would you like to play? There was no need to answer. We skidded to the heavy-lidded chest in the back hall full of the Captain and Mrs Hollings' discarded finery, presumably also shipped from Home. I wore black velvet and a solar topee. Beryl sailed along the concrete paths in front of me trailing green lace, clumping along in ankle strap Minnie Mouse shoes, her head high as we progressed towards Making Up, our discontinuous unwritten lives beneath the lemon tree.

— Where had we got to? she asked on arrival, adjusting the set of the peplum above her knees.

— You're still in the cave, I said. — I haven't broken free yet.

— Well hurry up, said Beryl, sitting down in butter box confinement.

Our real life was carefully hidden at school. We were in the same class, with Miss Lynksey who taught me right from left and ran a ballot for the class monitor. We voted according to sex and sycophancy. I voted for Beryl who voted for Ann Henare who voted for Glenys Ashwood who voted for the next girl up.

My visits to the Hollings increased in frequency. Happy, wreathed in night smells, we lay in our narrow beds telling. — I'll tell if you tell. I flaunted my double-jointed thumbs. Beryl skited her tap steps. We swapped comics, *Dick Tracey* for *Phantom*. We investigated Romance, our stomachs flat on the sun-baked verandah. ('She has dirtied her face to hide her beauty,' cried the Sultan. 'This shows intelligence. A rare thing in a slave girl'). We attached one end of a long rope to a hook on the verandah wall. — You turn, bossed Beryl. I swung the other end yelling — Apple jelly jam tart/Tell me the name of your sweetheart/A,B,C,D . . .

14

Beryl jumped, then tripped sprawling on the hot wood at M. — Mervyn, I squealed, — Mervyn Colley's your boy. Mervyn with purple painted school sores who squinted in the front row and still couldn't see. Beryl's bush of black hair shook as she leapt at me. I turned to flee and cannoned into Mrs Holling's wet apron.

— Elaine, she gasped, winded. — Beryl, look who's here.

We stared at my cousin Diane in her frock with apples on it, five years younger, smiling and golden. We untied the rope, hooked it round her shoulders and ran her deep through the garden behind the garage to the lemon tree. Her cheeks were pinker than ever from the enforced gallop. She glowed with pleasure, proud to play with the big kids. Beryl moved to me, stiff fingers shielding her secret.

— The Ward of the Sultan is in our power! she hissed.

— Yes!

— We'll tie her up.

— Yes! Yes!

— For ever. Beryl's usually pale face was scarlet. My legs were hot with excitement. My cousin smiled, safe as houses. Beryl seized one end of the rope and we twirled the captive around twisting and tugging, one at each end. — She is our slave. — Yes! — For ever! My heart was bonging, too big for its space.

— She can take your father's toast in! I screamed. Diane's smile faltered. She tried to reach out a hand to me. Beryl slapped it back and tugged harder on the cords. — Eelaine, panted my cousin.

— And help him on with his leg! shouted Beryl.

— No! squealed the terrified child. We dragged the struggling kicking bawling four year old to the post of the clothes line and slammed her against it, my knee in her stomach my hands busy while Beryl loosed and retied the rope. We cobbled the ends together, our fingers tense and eager. My pants were wet with mob violence, my throat harsh with blood lust. Diane's eyes never left my face.

15

— Eeelaine! Eeelaine! she sobbed. 'The bleating of the kid
excites the tiger.'

— Shut up I said, my face stiff with rejection.

— Mum! screamed my cousin with the hysterical despair
of the betrayed.

— Belt up! said Beryl, her hands tugging at the knots.

— Or we'll sock you! I yelled, jumping up and down in
damp chilling delight.

All this Morris Baker and I remember as we sit facing each
other in the still room and our relationship shifts and slides
and does not resettle. Author and reader, admired and
admirer have vanished from my cousin's sparsely-furnished
lovingly-furbished spare room. The room is empty. There
is no sound.

Morris Baker's strong left hand, the nails pink and curved,
touches her powdered cheek. The hairs on her arms are
no longer dark like they used to be. Her ear lobes are rounded
and puffy, modelled from play dough, the chunky gold
earrings too heavy for old ears. Her handkerchief is a tight
ball.

— Do you remember . . . says Morris Baker.

— Yes, I say. Yes, I do.

Up the River with Mrs Gallant

Mr Levis invited them to call him Des. And this is Arnold he said.

Mr Kent said Hi Arnold.

Mrs Kent said that she was pleased to meet him.

Mrs Gallant said Hullo, Arnold.

Mr Gallant said Good morning.

Mr Borges said nothing.

Des said that if they just liked to walk down to the landing stage Arnold would bring the boat down with the tractor.

Mrs Gallant said wasn't Mr Gallant going to leave the car in the shade.

Mr Gallant said that if Mrs Gallant was able to tell him where the shade from one tree was going to be for the next six hours he would be happy to.

Mr Kent said that he was going to give it a burl anyway and reparked the Falcon beneath the puriri.

Mrs Kent told Mrs Gallant that she and Stan were from Hamilton.

Mrs Gallant told Mrs Kent that she and Eric were from Rotorua.

Mrs Kent said that she had a second cousin in Rotorua. Esme. Esme. She would be forgetting her own head next.

And that she supposed she should wait for Stan but what the hell.

Mrs Gallant smiled at Mr Borges.

Mr Borges nodded.

At the landing stage Des said that he would like them to take turns sitting in the front and perhaps the ladies?

Mrs Kent remarked that the landing stage looked a bit ass over tip.

Arnold said that the landing stage was safe as houses and would the lady get into the boat.

Mrs Kent said Where was Stan.

Mr Kent said Here.

Mrs Kent asked Mr Kent where he had got to. She hopped across the landing stage, climbed onto the boat and into one of the front seats. She said that it wasn't too lady like but that she would be right.

Mrs Gallant followed.

Mr Kent and Mr Gallant climbed into the next row.

Des said that Arnold was on the Access Training Scheme and doing very well but it was difficult to fit in the hundred hours river time in a business like this and that he hoped that the customers would have no objection if Arnold came with them and drove the boat back because of the hundred hours.

Mrs Kent said that she would be delighted anytime.

Mr Kent said Well.

Mr Gallant asked how many passengers the boat was licensed for.

Des said that it was licensed for seven passengers.

Mrs Gallant smiled.

Mr Borges said nothing.

Arnold said Good on them, climbed into the boat and sat in the back row with Mr Borges. Mr Borges smiled.

Des started the motor and picked up the microphone. He said that the river was approximately ninety miles long and had been called the Rhine Of New Zealand. It had been used as a waterway since the time of the first Maoris.

Perhaps the busiest time on the river, he said, was the end of the nineteenth century and the beginning of the twentieth until the Main Trunk was completed. River boats plied, freight and passengers were transported in thousands and in all that time there were only two deaths which must be something of a record.

Mr Gallant said that he hoped that it would stay that way.

Des invited him to come again.

Mrs Kent said that Mr Gallant was only kidding.

Mr Gallant said No he wasn't.

Mrs Gallant said Eric.

Des said that he was born and brought up on the river. He had lived on the river all his life and he knew the river like the back of his hand and his aim was for every one of his passengers to learn more about this beautiful river which was steeped in history.

Mr Kent said that Des would do him.

Mrs Kent said Hear Hear.

Mr Borges, Mr Gallant and Arnold said nothing.

Mrs Gallant said that it was a lovely day.

Des said that she wasn't running as sweet as usual, probably a few stones up the grille.

Mrs Gallant asked What did that mean.

Des said Stones you know up the grille.

Mrs Gallant said that she realised that.

Mr Gallant smiled.

Mrs Kent said that they had a lovely day for it anyhow.

Des said they certainly had and to take a look at the flying fox across the river. He explained that the alignment of the posts was very important indeed.

Mr Gallant said that it would be.

Des said that otherwise she could come across but she wouldn't go back. On the other hand if it was wrong the other way she would go back but she wouldn't come across.

Mr Gallant said Exactly.

Mr Kent said it was all Dutch to him Ooh Pardon.

19

Mrs Kent said that the young man wasn't Dutch and that Stan needn't worry.

Mr Kent said Then what was he?

Mrs Kent said that yes the day certainly was a cracker.

Mrs Gallant smiled.

Des said that the cooling system wasn't operating as per usual either. Usually she stayed at twenty. That was what he liked her at. Twenty.

Mrs Gallant said that it was at seventy now was it not.

Des said Yes it was.

Mrs Gallant said Oh.

Mr Gallant laughed.

Des said that they certainly would like Pipiriki.

Mrs Kent said That was for sure.

Des moored the boat at the Pipiriki landing stage. Everyone climbed out. Des put a large carton on an outdoor table and said they could help themselves to tea or coffee.

Mrs Gallant said that she and Eric would only need one teabag between them as they both took tea very weak without milk.

Des said that Mrs Gallant needn't worry as he had provided two tea bags each per person as usual.

Mr Gallant said that she was only trying to help.

Mrs Kent asked if there was a toilet.

Arnold pointed up the path.

Des said that after lunch they should go up and look at Pipiriki. Pipiriki House had once been a world famous hotel. It had burned down in 1959. He said to have a good look at the shelter and to go around the back as there were some flush toilets.

Mrs Kent said that now Des told her and they both laughed.

Mrs Gallant said What shelter.

Des said A shelter for tourists you know trampers, that sort of thing.

Everyone liked Pipiriki very much. After an hour they climbed back into the boat.

Mr Kent said that he wished some of those activists could see all those kids happy and swimming.

Mr Gallant said Why?

Mr Kent said to look at that one jumping there. That he hadn't a care in the world.

Mr Gallant said that that was hardly the point.

Mrs Gallant said Eric.

Mr Gallant said Hell's delight woman.

Mr Borges smiled.

Mrs Kent said that they used to live near Cambridge but that they had moved in to Hamilton when the boy took over.

Mrs Gallant said Was that right, and that she wished they had been able to land at Jerusalem.

Arnold said that he could go a swim.

Des said that he had been going to have a good look at her yesterday but that he hadn't had a break for so long and that he just hadn't felt like it.

No one said anything.

Des said that anyway he had had another booking in the end as things had turned out.

The boat leapt and bucked high in the air.

Mrs Kent said Ooops.

Des said that that showed you what happened if you let your concentration slip even for a second with a jetty. She had hit a stump.

Mr Gallant laughed.

Arnold asked if the Boss would like him to take over.

Des and Arnold laughed.

Mrs Gallant said to look at that kingfisher.

Mrs Kent said Where.

Mrs Gallant said There. That Mrs Kent was too late. That it had gone.

Des pointed out many points of interest and said that no she certainly wasn't going too good.

Mrs Gallant said that hadn't the temperature gauge gone up to eighty or was she wrong.

21

Des said that no she was not wrong and that he had better give her a breather and stopped the boat. He said it was probably the temperature of the water, it being a hot day.

Nobody said anything. The boat rocked, silent on the trough of its own waves. The sun shone.

Des said that that should have cooled her down a bit and started the boat.

The temperature gauge climbed to seventy.

Des said that that was more like it and that there had been a Maori battle on that island between the Hau Hau supporters and the non-supporters.

Mr Gallant wondered why they had chosen an island.

Des said that Mr Gallant had him there and swung the boat into a shallow tributary of the river. He told Arnold that they had better check the grille and how would Arnold like a swim.

Arnold said that that would be no problem. He climbed around onto the bow of the boat and said that they would now see his beautiful body. He removed his shirt and told Mrs Gallant and Mrs Kent to control themselves.

Mrs Kent yelped.

Arnold faced the vertical cliff of the bank, presented his shorts clad buttocks and shook them.

Everyone laughed except Mr Gallant and Mr Borges.

Mr Borges stood up quickly, took a photograph of Arnold's back view, and sat down again.

Arnold jumped into the water and swam to the back of the boat. Des fumbled beneath his feet and handed the passengers various pieces of equipment for Arnold to poke up the grille. The male passengers handed the things on to Arnold with stern efficiency.

After some time Arnold said that he had found three stones up the grille.

Des said that that was good.

Arnold said that they were not big buggers though.

Des said Never mind.

Arnold handed the equipment back into the boat and did a honeypot jump from the shallow water into a deep pool.

Mr Kent said See?

Arnold swam to the bow of the boat and heaved himself into the boat.

Mr Borges took a photograph of Arnold's front view.

Mrs Gallant said that they were lucky that Arnold had come with them.

Mrs Kent said that Mrs Gallant could say that again and would the boat go better now that Arnold had removed the stones.

Des said that he hoped so.

Mr Gallant laughed.

They stopped several times on the return trip for the boat to cool down and as she was not going too well Des sometimes had to make several sweeps before she could pick up enough speed for her to lift up over the rapids. Des said that normally at this stage, when she was less than half full of gas he could fling her about all over the place no sweat.

Mr Gallant said that they must be thankful for small mercies.

Des swung the boat in a wide spraying circle and pulled into the jetty at the old flour mill. They climbed the hill, Des carrying the afternoon tea carton. After tea Des said that he would tell them about the old flour mill and the river in general. Everyone expressed interest. They trooped into the warm shadowy old building and Des began.

After half an hour Mrs Kent asked whether Des would mind if she sat down.

Des said that although perhaps it was technically more correct to call them river boats he still thought of them as steamers though strictly speaking they weren't steamers for long.

Mrs Kent sat down.

Mrs Gallant sat down.

Mr Kent looked as though he was going to cry.

Mr Gallant closed his eyes.

Arnold sat outside in the shade.

Mr Borges joined him.

After three quarters of an hour Des said that he hoped they had all learned something of the river.

They climbed down to the river in silence.

Des said that as she wasn't the best perhaps if Mrs Gallant and Mr Kent would like to sit in front.

Mr Gallant muttered something about sensible arrangement of ballast.

Mrs Kent asked Des why.

Arnold said it was because he liked the good-looking girls in the back with him.

Mrs Kent told Arnold to get away and climbed nimbly into the back seat.

Mrs Gallant said nothing.

They set off with Des at the wheel. The temperature gauge rose above eighty. Des asked the passengers to look around their feet for a tool which would enable Arnold to take another poke up the grille without getting out of the boat.

Mrs Gallant said that there was a pipe thing here if that was any help.

Mrs Kent gave a startled cry and said What was that smoke.

Mr Gallant said that that was steam.

Mrs Kent said that it was red hot that pipe thing there.

Mr Gallant said that he was not at all surprised.

Arnold said that she would be right.

Des said that she had better have another cool off and stopped the boat.

The boat limped to the original landing jetty two hours later than planned. The passengers collected their belongings without comment and trailed up the hill.

Des told Arnold that he could bring the boat up.

Arnold said that Des was the Boss.

Mrs Gallant remarked that it had been a very interesting day and that wasn't the river beautiful.

Mrs Kent said that yes it was but that she had felt so sorry for the poor chap.

Mr Gallant said God in Heaven.

Mrs Gallant remarked that she saw that Mr Kent's car was in the shade.

Mr Gallant said that it probably had not been for the first six hours.

Mrs Gallant said that that remark was typical absolutely typical.

Mrs Kent said that they used to have Jerseys but the boy had switched to Friesians.

Mr Kent said that he had been happy enough in Jerseys but that there you were.

Mrs Kent said that they just want to be different and that it was quite understandable.

Mr Kent said that he had never said it wasn't.

Mr Borges said nothing.

Arnold appeared on the tractor, pulling the boat on its trailer. He parked it in the shed and appeared with a Visitors' Book. He invited the passengers to make their crosses.

Everyone laughed except Mr Gallant and Mr Borges.

Des said that he would give her an overhaul tomorrow that was for sure.

Mrs Kent signed the book and wrote Lovely day under Comments.

Mr Kent signed and wrote Ditto.

Mr Gallant signed his name only.

Mr Borges signed and wrote Sweden.

Mrs Gallant missed the signing. She stumped across the bleached grass and stood gazing at the river.

It said nothing.

Shanties

I sit in my caravan in the El Dorado caravan park and I
think I am a very lucky woman. I think of those shanties
we saw on the roadside.

I am very fond of my caravan. The man I bought it from
painted it himself. He was a professional house painter of
the old school, no spraying. The brush marks don't show
or anything but it looks, well it would have been better
sprayed. It is the shape of a Walt Disney cloud, rounded
at both ends. But blue. Inside it is punk pink. Very compact
if a bit tatsy but caravans often are, they seem to bring
out the kitsch. The vendor showed me his product most
meticulously. He pulled out the drawers. He unrolled the
awning. We squatted together, heads close as children with
jokes while we inspected the underpinnings. I kicked the
tyres. He was selling it because he'd bought it as a spare
room for his daughter who didn't come. She was in Brisbane
and she wrote to say she was coming, but . . . His voice
trailed away. I didn't pursue it. I couldn't do anything and
I didn't want to start thinking negative thoughts about my
elliptical pie in the sky. I could see he was glad to get rid
of it though.

The caravan park is well run by the caretaker, Mr Kelson. Most of the residents are long-term. We're long-term they say. Nothing fly-by-night with us though that remains unsaid. Some are so long-term they have pretend fences which define their territory. Mr Laski's is a one foot high white picket. One has a path to the door bordered with matching river stones painted white. Many of the homes have names emblazoned on their sleek sides. Rio Bella Vista has a glimpse of the river. Roll Your Own next door to me will never cruise again because Mrs Millrod is a widow and Cyril did the driving. Mrs Millrod is the victim of some crippling disease. She is very small and has to turn her head sideways to smile up at me. For some reason this makes even her 'Good morning Julie' seem wise, knowing. She is uncomplaining and cheerful in her little girl dresses and doesn't ask questions. I am thinking of painting Run Away on my mobile home but would they get it? Or El Deserto? Better just to say my husband . . . Yes, well, what? My husband and I . . . Some sort of caravan park Queen's Message for God's sake. The thing is, it's not only the things that happen, it's the explanations required. The new persona which must be created, the screen relit behind which I dance.

*

The hotel suite was vast. Mike tipped the man who delivered the luggage and turned to her, stroking a hand over his seal coat hair. She was bouncing on the enormous double bed in her petticoat, her shoes abandoned in the middle of the room, their heels angled. — Bit of a scream, she called. — What? he said. — The whole thing. Us. Here. Everything. He lay down on the other side of the King Size, a yard across the furrows of the quilted bedspread. She stopped bouncing and snatched her narrow feet to sit cross-legged, calves flat on the bed, supple and trim as a worked out Jane Fonda. — I mean *look* at it! She stared at the muted pastels of the overstuffed chairs, the decorator prints on the walls of the opulent anonymous room. — It's so huge . . . We could hold a levee why not? Her hand covered her mouth in a caricature of stifled laughter. She laughed at her jokes, her faux pas, at bloody life itself. He dropped his shoulders and breathed out.

— Julie.

— Yes?

Phrases slid into his mind. — I've slaved for it. — For God's sake, woman. — Why don't you . . . — Why can't you . . .

Were abandoned. — Nothing.

Her head lifted, scenting the frustration behind his silence.

— The firm's paying, he said.

— I didn't mean *that*, she said. The corners of her mouth twitched. The attempt to suppress her laughter, to humour him as though he was a fractious child, infuriated him further. He rolled over to the edge of the vast bed. He should go through the draft of his speech. See Brett. He loosened his tie. Yawned. The air conditioning wasn't perfect. — Don't forget the laundry, he muttered. — No. She was reading the house magazine of the hotel chain. — Listen to this. The Hotel Ponceroo is situated in central downtown Washington with easy access to . . . Can it be central and downtown at the same time? He closed his eyes. — Yes, he said. — Yes, it can, he told the darkness.

He jolted upright at her shriek, his heart lurching. She stood at the window, her feet half buried in the carpet, a six foot bath sheet wrapped around her body. Her hair was wet, her mouth hung open with delight not terror. She was pointing out the window. — Look at that! He dragged himself off the bed and shambled over. She had pulled back one of the curtains on which peonies, birds of paradise and chinese temples melded in corals and greens. It revealed a concrete service area lined with garbage cans. A rangy cat stalked its beat, planting each pad with care. Mike stared down, clutching the window sill. — What's wrong with it? he said. — No, no. She pointed again. — *That*! A neon sign on the roof of the building opposite flashed red white red white across the bleak scene. — Eddie's Condoms! Eddie's Condoms! Eddie's Condoms! — Isn't that *marvellous*! she cried. He stared at the sign, his eyelids heavy as safety curtains, hating her. — It's just so . . . Oh I can't explain. Like that weight lifter who 'rips his glutes'. So *marvellous*! she said.

*

I have been lucky also in finding a job. This is a country town and it has problems and the worst is lack of employment. People stand around. There is an air of . . . decay is too strong a word. Even the multi-coloured plastic streamers above the used car lots seem listless. The place used to bustle and throb with energy like a farm generator I knew. Mr Barber made his own electricity which seemed a God-like activity. A generator crouched at the back of his garage waiting to stutter into creation.

I have a job in the local canning factory. I sit with the other women at the ever coming conveyor belt as the peas roll by and we remove shreds of leaves, tendrils, all the waste scraps of a pea crop. All day our hands move rhythmically in sweeping arcs, our fingers are nimble and selective, our heads are turbanned in green. We spy for purity. We judge. We are efficient and sharp-eyed. Nothing extraneous escapes us. Once I found a feather in a can of chicken soup but that was in another country.

I am not reticent with the other women. Fouled-up relationships flow by like the peas, but nobody picks at them. There is a lot of laughter as we sit on the splay-legged plastic chairs in the canteen. We had to help Em up the day she christened the conveyor belt the steel eel.

*

The aircraft slipped down onto the runway. He glanced across her and nodded. A good landing. His smile was that of a fellow conspirator, eye contact, closed lips. She smiled

29

back then began stowing her mess of clutter in a string kit of all things. As the plane braked to a stop a team of uniformed workmen ran onto the tarmac to align the steps. They ran bent double as though intent on avoiding detection. Three young women in green lily gowns held ropes of flower garlands. A band struck up an oompah of welcome as Brett appeared to check the cabin luggage. His upper lip twitched beneath the ragged sandy moustache. — And the little one. Right then? He beamed at them, his face proud. The door opened and the heat blasted in. Mike bent his head, then straightened quickly to run down the aircraft steps, hand outstretched to clasp the hand of the senior member of the group waiting to greet him. Julie followed, her linen suit a crumpled disaster, the orange string kit bumping her knee at every step. — I think the aircraft's got a flat tyre, she told the welcoming committee.

Unlike Washington, the air conditioning was faultless. Brett was taking notes, the ballpoint in his left hand pecking at a small pad. — Oh yes, he said. — One more thing. The helicopter. Doors on or off? They want to know which you prefer. — Oh. Off I think. Mike glanced across at Julie who was upended over a suitcase on the floor. — Definitely, she said. She straightened up from her head down bottom up scrabbling and looked distractedly around the suite.

— What is it now? said Mike.
— My blue belt.
He looked at the easy-care non-iron hanging around her like a sack. Her lack of vanity used to fascinate him. He dismissed the thought quickly. — It doesn't need a belt, he lied.
— It does, but what the hell. The jungle won't care.
— We're not going to the jungle. I told you we're . . .
— You said I think we should go into the jungle and I said speak for yourself and you said . . .
— That was yesterday. We went. You didn't.
— I know I didn't. She stood on one foot as though

30

practising balance. — No jungle?

— We go *over* the jungle, said Brett, ever helpful.

— Ah. She raked a hand through her hair. — It's just the snakes.

— The snakes aren't going to bounce up at you.

— Not to a helicopter. No. She sounded genuinely amused. Probably was he thought sourly.

— No doors eh? That's great. So what is it today?

— Why don't you read the flaming programme?

— Because I've lost the flaming programme. She smiled. — One of our programmes is missing. Shot down with the belt.

His shoulders sagged. — Today we visit a hydroelectric project. We drive to the airport. We fly for two hours to an outlying island . . .

She looked puzzled. — No doors?

— God in heaven! The two hours is in a fixed-wing aircraft. The helicopter is just the last half hour. He snatched the programme from his open briefcase and flapped it at her, jabbing an accusing finger at the print. — See!

— Yes, she said.

The drive to the airport seemed endless. The driver manoeuvred through the chaos of city traffic onto a motorway which lead through an industrial hinterland of grey. The grass verge beneath the hoardings was lined with squatter's shanties built from straw mats, cardboard, an occasional length of corrugated iron. Nobody was visible. They must be at work. But where were the children? She turned to ask Mike, as if he would know. His eyes were closed.

— Mike?

— Nnnn?

— Nothing.

The car sped on.

She tried to work out the advertisements, most of them obvious. Delighted women gazed with rapture at cakes of soap. Children stretched eager arms to toys forever beyond their reach. A giant Pink Panther gesticulated with writhing neon limbs above a garage. Factories became fewer.

They left the motorway and drove through a suburb. Tropical trees soared above them, their branches touching across the road. Weathered stone walls covered in cascading pink and orange flowered creepers hid the houses beyond. Women with straw brooms whisked the unblemished footpaths. The driver glanced at her in the rear vision mirror and smiled his gap-toothed smile.

Most of the party slept in the fixed-wing aircraft. Mouths hung open, an occasional snorting snore woke its sleeper. Technical magazines slipped to the floor. Mike's rough pad was open on his knees as he stared at the jungle searching for words. Julie slept beside him, her head heavy on his shoulder. Eventually Brett moved forward touching the back of each seat. — Ten minutes, he said.

The reception at the tiny airport was a miniature of their arrival in the country two days before. Heat struck the tarmac and was reflected back. Officials greeted them, wives were introduced. Everyone smiled; nervous smiles, hopeless smiles, smiles of jaw-cracking intensity. Different slender young women placed garlands around the same bent necks. A large corsage of white and pink orchids was pinned to the front of Julie's sack-like garment by the smallest garland lady. Photographs were taken. They moved across the shimmering runway to the helicopter which squatted nearby. — Outside or in? Mike asked her. — Outside. The pragmatism of helicopters; up, along, down. No messing about.

The young pilot checked their safety belts, smiling and gentle. The smile snapped off, his face was blank and tough as he climbed into his seat and started the engine. They lifted rapidly. Julie stared down at the viridian landscape. People below pointed and waved, paddy fields became patches, farmers working on the terraced hillsides became toys then disappeared. The wind rushed by tugging and ripping at her corsage as she leant out. After a few minutes the whole thing broke loose and hurtled downwards. Her laughter tossed after it. — I've lost it! she shouted at Mike. — What? — Never mind!

She thought of the falling flowers. Imagined them drifting down, spiralling gently till they brushed the ground at the feet of a farmer, his wife, a spellbound child. Undamaged, a gift of no value, but perfect. A sign. In reality of course they would hurtle downwards, self-destructing, crashing to a pulp. The wire could damage even. Mike leant over to her. — *What've* you lost, he yelled.

*

— What're you doing at Christmas, Julie? Em asks on the way back from the canteen. What I'm doing at Christmas is holing up, burrowing deep as a mutton bird into El Deserto, so I have to think quickly.

— Uh, I say for time. — Come to us, she says. I want to tell her how it happened but there is no time and anyway I can't remember. I want to tell her I can't remember.

I remember leaving, I can see the shape of the broken bit on the bottom step as I lugged my suitcase, but I can't remember a lot of it. We had a major row I remember that. We didn't often have them. We were more subtle. After ten years we knew how to slip the knife in. Expert anatomists, we operated with wrist-turning speed, our triumph the shock on the face of the loved one, the lover who didn't know he/she had been stabbed till the pain. We used the tools of the intimate; old sour jokes, resurrected pomposities, small meannesses. You can't hone those weapons on strangers.

I can't remember how it started even. It was the Sunday after we got back from that place. I can see the colours. Dark blue sweatshirt, old white shorts. Something about fruit juice cartons and how you can never get into the things. I can see the orange oblong in his hand as he shouts at me. See myself crouched behind the table, clutching the life-support formica. Hear the noise ricocheting around the Living Decor Kitchen as I duck his blistering rage and slam it back.

Mr Kelson, the caretaker, is employed by the absentee owner. I admire Mr Kelson because he is so tidy. He is neat and trim, his work shorts knife-pleated. Rubbish is anathema to him. If it is small enough he stabs it with a spike then scrapes the spike clean against the side of a small cart he made himself. It is almost a child's trolley but not quite. He trims the edges of the grass alongside the concrete paths with a wheel like a giant pastry cutter on a long handle then stows the shavings in his cart. Again it looks almost fun but not quite. Mr Kelson shakes me by the hand and wishes me a Merry Christmas. His hand is hard and bony, cool to the touch. He wears a cap with Hawaii Hotcha printed on it in red, a gift from his son who has made it (lifestyle-wise) in the States. Mr Kelson shoves it back on his head, the yellow duck's bill peak aims at the blazing sky. He looks at me thoughtfully. — I hope it goes off all right for you, he says. — Christmas and that.

Christmas is over now so I am relaxed, lying prone on my pink bed reading an article about where people go to buy the best of things they wish to buy in Auckland, when Mike comes up my step. I fall upright. — How'd you know I was here? I hiss. We stare at each other, two cornered animals.
    — Oh God, he says.
    — Christmas is over, I say.
    He looks blank. — Christmas?
    I have been wary over Christmas.
    — All that food, he says still staring.
    My mind skitters, skids, runs down. I hear my voice.
— Where did you go?
    — Sandra's.

I believe him. Sandra the sister, the wife and mother, presiding calm and munificent over mountains of hot food, her hands busy with portions, her eyes begging seconds from her torpid husband, her tense skinny children.

My knees start to shake. I flop onto my bed. Mike sits on the divan. Our knees almost touch. His slip-on shoes are new, shiny and black as jackboots. A blowfly buzzes, flinging itself at the tiny window. I open the window and flop it out.

— Get out, I say to Mike.

There is a knock on the door. We stop shouting. Mike looks at me. My house. I open the door. Mr Kelson stands outside. Beside him, no higher than his chest, is Mrs Millrod, her sideways face worried, her hands clasped tight against her flowered front.

— Everything O.K. then Julie? says Mr Kelson.

— Fine. Fine, I say. — This is my husband Mike. Mrs Millrod my neighbour. Mr Kelson the caretaker.

Mike is already on his feet. He shakes Mr Kelson's cool hand. He steps down onto the beaten grass to greet Mrs Millrod. Her joy beams up at him. Mrs Millrod. Mrs Millrod.

Conversation is relaxed. Mike admires the condition of El Dorado. Mr Kelson says it's not easy with the casuals. Mike says he can understand that. Mrs Millrod smiles. They leave soon, after more handshakes, more smiles. Their departure is muted, tactful.

I have to say something . . . — Do you remember the shanties by the motorway in that awful place?

The pupils of his eyes have contracted in the sun.

— I didn't mean it, he says. — I didn't mean it.

The hand on my shoulder weighs a kilo.

— Julie, he says.

I am tired beyond words. I am drowning in a deep river of sleep. I almost yawn. The effort of swallowing the thing exhausts me further.

—Forget it, I say. — Forget it.

Poojah

When I was a small child our neighbour Miss Messerson took me by the hand and led me into a large bedroom in her house next door where she lifted me up to show me the body of her mother as she thought I would like to see her as Mother looked so beautiful. I have little memory of this experience other than a sensation of wishing to be elsewhere. Not an uncommon childhood sensation.

It surfaced, for example, every Christmas when we were taken to do poojah to Baby Jesus at an ivy-covered house in the Cashmere hills. The house belonged to Mrs Carter. The best part was the stone frog on the entrance porch, more throttled by ivy each year, but available for stroking if requested. It had to be sought out by Mrs Carter's daughter Mildred.

We shuffled in with our parents, my father solemn, my mother smiling. We wore our best clothes which I could recognise today. For several years I wore a white summer jersey knitted in moss stitch embroidered at the plain yoke with pink worm roses, and a white pleated skirt. My brother wore blue shorts, a white shirt, a miniature navy blue spotted bow tie and the expression of an enraged bull. He was a heller, my brother, and very beautiful. His curls rioted, his

36

eyes blazed, and his dark lashes were so long they became a nuisance later when he had to wear glasses. Perhaps that was part of his problem, but impaired vision or not, Duncan was 'difficult'. We were both under duress at poojah. He from rage, I from embarrassment.

When we had all assembled, shuffled our feet, found the frog, we mooched in and greeted Mrs Carter. The room into which we were herded was small and dark, the heavy velvet curtains pulled against the blazing sun. A huge Christmas tree touched the gabled roof, the air was thick with incense. Mrs Carter, whose ankles were so swollen she could scarcely walk, sat filling a wide chair in the shadows to the left of the tree. I know now because I have been told that she was a wise, well-educated woman of a kindly disposition. I saw the smile but it was no help. She was the spider occupant and we were trapped in deep scented misery.

Mildred Carter did the marshalling. When I heard of 'marshalling yards' during the war I thought of Mildred. What age was she? Forty, fifty? We had no way of knowing and anyhow it was irrelevant. She was grey all over. Her grey hair sprung outwards from her small head. Her dress was also grey. She wore no make-up and her smile wore thin as the afternoon progressed. But she had a fair turn of speed which she demonstrated whenever Duncan or Evan Morrison made a break for it. One or the other (they never combined their talents as far as I can remember) would fling himself down the parched grass slope, screaming, but there was no escape. Cornered, they would be 'led' back by Mildred, who never even puffed, and handed over to their respective mothers for mopping up while their respective fathers stared thoughtfully into the middle distance and I wished to be somewhere else.

Day after day, week after week through the hot summer the ceremony continued. There were usually no more than one or two other families present with their offspring as Mrs Carter disliked crowds. Mr Morrison, large and jokey,

was always present when we were with his gentle wife
and Evan; six years of skin and bone and quivering tension.
Sometimes the bland Parkins were there with their stolid
twins who seemed unravaged by the proceedings. Sometimes the creaking Dr Perry and his sad wife, and daughter
Jane who we had to be nice to. — *Why* Mum? — Sssh
Duncan.

— Everybody here. A statement of fact from Mildred,
not a question. She adjusted the needle of the gramophone
and the choir of King's College Cambridge burst into the
heat and incense with the injunction *Oh come all ye faithful.*
The parents stood with their backs to the wall, their children
either rebellious, or resigned or calm (and who could tell
which). Sometimes a baby cried, always Evan whimpered.

— Now, said Mildred. — Who will poojah first? You
Patricia? Good girl. Patricia would toss back her thick hot
plait, take the censer from Mildred's outstretched hands and
kneel in front of the nativity scene assembled at the base
of the Christmas tree. There was a camel with a nodding
head. Nothing was to scale. The Christ Child lay big as
a shepherd. A lamp was the same size as a Nubian King,
a tiger smaller than a lamb. Styles differed also. Attenuated
figures handcarved in Germany stood or lay alongside
strange garish-coloured animals from Mrs Carter's East. I
would like to say that this eclecticism symbolised for me
the whole world but this was not so. I thought it a mess,
and a hot mess and I wished to be gone, especially when
Mildred turned to me with a smile and said — Beth? Assisted
by a poke between the shoulder blades from my mother
I fell on my knees. I realise now that poojah is a Sanskrit
word meaning a ritual act of worship. We were meant to
make the sign of the cross, then, helped by Miss Carter,
strike the censer three times against its base — and say
in clear tones, — Happy Birthday, Baby Jesus. I never
achieved the clear tones but I did better than Evan who
panicked yearly. — Happy slappy, happy . . . Maam, he
screamed, stumbling to his feet, the smoking censer

abandoned on the carpet to be snatched up by the nearest adult as he blundered to bury his shamed head against his mother's thighs, to feel the stroking hand, the Sssh Evan. It's all right. There, honey, there.

Duncan did better. In later years when I was still longing for extinction he grasped the censer and made poojah with grace and dignity. I merely thought he'd sold out.

Tea happened afterwards in another shadowed room. Why was it called the House of Sunshine, when the sun was so rigorously excluded? We followed Mrs Carter, who hobbled on two sticks. We trailed through dark passages, up a flight of steps to the dining room to be greeted by the black variety of Christmas cake which no child will eat and animal biscuits which we considered beneath us but ate anyway. I suppose our parents were there. Evan Morrison usually pinched me in a friendly way on my behind. Though perhaps I am confused, it may not have been friendly at that age, but he is not alive to ask. Once we escaped and rolled down the bank clutching our yellow pigs and pink lions watched by the startled Parkins. But only once.

What was it all about? A simple celebration of the Adoration by two devout High Anglican churchwomen, in which we were all invited to join, especially the children. But why poojah? Had they lived in India? Presumably, but why the amalgam? And why were we never told?

All I know is that when we piled into the stifling car and my father drove home, his eyes straight ahead, and my mother sang:

> I fell into a basket of eggs
> And all the yellow splashed over my legs
> Yip I addy I ay, I ay
> Yip I addy I ay

I have never felt happier in my life.

The Girls

All the girls could kill. Their father taught them. — Stand astride grip with the knees yank the head, knife in. Speed's the thing. They smell blood.

All the girls did too. Blood, the sour smell of concrete and later the stench of guts. A gantry with a pulley was positioned above the sump. There was a tap with a length of blue hose attached. A naked light bulb hung from the ceiling, the shadows were sharp. Years later when Ellespie saw an interrogation scene in an old black-and-white she smelled the shed and moved her lover's hand from her thigh. His beard loomed. — What's wrong? She shook her head and stared at the face of the victim which filled the screen.

The killing shed was an exact square of concrete blocks. It squatted beside the woolshed in direct line with house.

— Couldn't you screen it or something their mother said.

— Plant a bloody rose on if you like said their father but she never got round to it.

She came from Argyll, a small woman with thin ankles and tiny paw-like hands. He fell without volition, a sinker plummeting. She maddened him, called him insane names, seemed amused, teased him with distance and flair. Sometimes in despair he could almost imagine grabbing that red-blond bush of hair, twisting it at the back, jerking.

— You'll have to marry me Elspeth he said.

She did, and hated everything about the place: the mountains which lay too near, slanting in long diagonals against the sky; the trim little cottage which became less so as the hot pink paint faded to blush and the tide of grime mounted.

She chanted the Highland expatriate's song to herself, grinding it into her mind. 'Yet still the blood is strong, the heart is Highland. And we in dreams behold the Hebrides.' Except that the blood was not and the dream an ache in the mouth.

Why did she marry him then? She knew her own mind, a source of interest and pleasure to her, so why had she drifted into it? Not because he insisted, demanded, standing with legs tensed as though he might spring at her. — I don't think I love you, I mean . . . He slammed his hands together. — Love! Christ, I've got enough for a harem he said.

She tried with the girls. — I did try. She had dreamt of a romance in which she starred as Mother; of lovable infants tumbling at her feet, not four lean and hungry whippets. Shona, Fiona, Ellespie and Jean.

He slaved on the place which was barely a viable unit. Shona heard and told them. — The farm's barely a viable unit she whispered. Oh, they said. He was a hard worker. Elspeth, even her mother in a brief disastrous visit, granted him that dour colonial accolade. She watched him one evening as he fed the dogs from the dog tucker safe which stood on four legs beside the chopping board. His knife slashed and hacked, she could see it glinting in the dusk as the dogs strained at the ends of their chains, their barks screaming yelps, their leaping bodies twisted. He had been out since six that morning with one brief marauding stop at the house for food. Elspeth's mother watched in silence till each dog had been flung its share. She turned from

41

the window and plonked stiff-kneed on the flowered sofa, pulling the knitting needle from the coil of hair on her neck. — He's honest, he's a hard worker, you married him now get on with it she said.

Elspeth knew she had tried to shatter the cool mother tradition she had been born to. Had tried to break the mould, which unless smashed, sets each daughter in her mother's attitudes. As soon as she pushed each daughter out to scream its arrival into the world, she tried. She cuddled each newborn, as emaciated as a Christ child in a fifteenth century Dutch painting. She suckled each grabbing mouth. She smiled and cooed at each set of grey eyes which stared unblinkingly at the centre of her forehead. And she gave up.

She took to little rests. As long as the girls could remember mother had a rest each afternoon. After lunch, once she'd got him out of the house again. Shona, Fiona, Ellespie and Jean, called Jinny, learnt early that you got them out of the house, though Dad leapt always, his hand reaching for his yellow towelling hat from the top of the fridge as she stacked the dishes and covered them with a tea towel, tucking in the corners because of the blowies.

— Look after Jean she said as usual one day in the school holidays. — I'm going to have a rest.

— Ssssh Shona warned as they crept beneath the bedroom window.

— Ssssh snarled Fiona and Ellespie, lips contorted against wrinkled noses with the effort. Jinny picked up the cat which emitted the ghost of a burp. It followed them across the chaffy grass most afternoons to the woolshed where they played involved and hierarchical games. — And Jinny can be the baby they said. Jinny rebelled. She was punting her behind along the oiled floor beneath the wool sorters' table crooning to herself. Her scream brought them running. She had gouged her hand on the rusty shearing comb which hung from her palm. Shona yanked it out, blinked at the beads of blood welling to streams, picked up the hiccoughing

42

child and ran. She was half way across the home paddock before she remembered. When Elspeth came out she found them all waiting on the back step, Jinny asleep in her sister's sharp arms, a stained tea towel around the hand.

— Why didn't you wake me!

— Shona's pinched face was blank. — You were having a Rest. You said!

— Mad . . . Mad.

Ellespie wanted to know what her mother did there. The girls were down at the creek after school, hunting for koura and she was sick of it, turning over stones and nothing there. — I want to go to the toilet she said. — Go here said Fiona. — No. She left them squatting in the chill water and ran up the hill, skipping the cowpats with precision. She dragged an empty apple box from the wash house, scrambled onto it and peered in. Her eyes met those of her mother who lay on her side of the bed, eyes open wide, wide. Ellespie toppled off the box and ran. Not even reading!

This one's the reader, Dad told Miss Pennelly, his hand on Ellespie's shoulder at school evenings to discuss progress. Their mother had gone too, originally.

— The Scotch, not Scottish, Scotch, have always known the importance of Education. Their public school education, and I mean *public*, is the best in the world. Bar none she told them firmly. — My mother is Scotch said Ellespie. — Scottish corrected Miss Pennelly. Ellespie let her have it.

But again she drifted from them. As it were. — You go Stan. Not tonight. I couldn't. She smiled up at him, her hair bright as sparks under the lamp though dimmed to faded ginger by day. He stood silent, hair slicked back. All ready. A muscle at the left side of his mouth jerked sideways as he shrugged into his whiskery sports coat. — All right you lot. Into the car. Not you Jinny. He lifted her from his feet, clenched her to him for a moment then handed the kicking child to Elspeth. — I want to go too! Legs

43

threshing, stick arms thrust upwards to deny purchase, Jinny
'performed'. Elspeth dropped her on the floor and picked
up the fair isle pattern as the door shut. She kept them
all in jerseys. — You're too little she told the sodden heap
bawling at her feet, her words drowned by the noise of
the Chrysler's gears crashing as it slammed down the track.

All the girls had to earn the right to work with him.
— I'll show you once. Right? he'd say, and they nodded.
Many things they knew because they had always known,
the same way they knew the door at the Farmer's Co-op
with the powder puff and mirror was theirs and Dad's the
one with the top hat. They knew which way each gate
opened, how to saddle up, whether it was a stray sheep
on the Tops, or that plant thing. How to feed out. He yelled
at them, his face twisted with rage, if they did anything
stupid. He never praised them, except Jinny. Occasionally
there was a wink as the last pen filled or they were cut
out in the sheds. Or as they jolted home in silence, the
scent of horse sweat heavy in the air. Killing was the last
thing he taught them, when they were about fifteen.
Ellespie was older. — I don't want to. I just don't want
to. Shona and Fiona had their own knives by now which
hung in the shed for when they were home.
— You don't have to Ellespie said her mother. She pressed
the palm of a hand against her back hair and pushed it
into shape.
— It's completely barbaric. I can't think how I ever allowed
it.
— You were probably having a rest Mum said Jinny.
— Don't cut your toast Jean. Break it.
— Why?
— Because. Elspeth demonstrated, her little paws tearing
the toast into large pieces.
— Of course she has to learn said their father. He was
puzzled, searching his wife's face for a clue. — What would
you do if I was ill?

44

Elspeth laughed, toast crumbs spurting from her lips.

— You! You wouldn't know how.

So Jinny the smallest, wiriest of them all learnt next. She reminded Ellespie of a game little Shorthorn calf. Tough orange curls bunched above her forehead. Although nimble, she seemed to stand four square, planted, her eyes steady in her pale face. She came back from the shed the first time in silence. — What was it like? whispered Ellespie. The grey eyes stared as though identifying her. Every freckle showed. — All right said Jinny.

When they left school Shona and Fiona flatted in town. Shona had style, an unexpected bonus. She cased her angular body in luminous trousers so tight they seemed painted on. Pelvic bones jutted either side of the concave dish of her stomach, her hair was swathed and hidden in scarves. Scarves like those worn by where-are-they-now actresses, though most are dead. Gloria Swanson say. She worked as a receptionist for two years (The Doctor will see you now) then married a young thruster from Christchurch who was giving the place a go to consolidate. Elspeth was slightly in awe of her eldest child. — Shona is a strong woman she said and you could make what you liked of it.

To the end of their days Shona and Fiona remained essential to each other. A matrix of trust and ambivalent memories united them. Happy? Unhappy? They discussed it endlessly. Spent hours telling each other things they already knew.

— Jinny was the rider of course said Shona.

— Oh of course said Fiona.

— I never was.

— No you weren't.

— Still it was fun wasn't it? tried Shona.

Fiona considered her verdict. — W-ell she said.

— I mean a lot of it.

— Oh yes, a *lot* of it.

They wrote frequent letters telling each other what the

recipient was doing, as though she had no way of knowing otherwise and would find the information useful. 'It is Thursday and you will be busy with the party for Doug's conference,' wrote Fiona. 'Wednesday so you'll have your spinning group,' replied Shona. Shona 'slipped away for a few days with Fif,' whenever she could manage to park the children.

— Do you think it would have been better if she'd left? Gone back? she asked one day, her breath puffing a drift of icing sugar from the top of Fiona's Blow Away Sponge. Fiona took a long sip of tea and replaced the cup in its saucer before replying.

— Well there you are. She sighed in elegaic sorrow for all remembered childhoods. — Who's to say? she said.

Fiona had married a high country farmer. She took her knife with her just in case. If Bruce or the shepherd or whoever couldn't kill. But of course it never was needed and rusted, wreathed in fluff behind scuffed shoes, deep in the back of the master wardrobe. Years later she wrapped it in newspaper and took it to the farm tip because of the children. It gave her a weird feeling as she flung it from her. That poem. King Arthur's sword, a hand coming up from the lake. The sword though would otherwise have sunk, whereas she had to clamber onto the uncertain surface of the tip to bury the knife. She covered it with over-age or unidentifiable objects from the deepfreeze clean out which had shared the wheelbarrow ride up from the house. Then lightened, at ease with the world, she pushed the empty barrow down the track in time for the school bus, singing *Jesu, joy of man's desiring* to the surrounding hills.

Shona's knife stayed in the shed. She seldom mentioned the farm. People were surprised. — You! On a farm?

Jinny used hers. She remained on the farm which she never had any intention of leaving. She was sweet as a nut, ageless as unticked time. As her mother drifted further further away she took over the housekeeping as well, such as it was. She slammed a joint of mutton in the oven when

46

necessary. She swept the kitchen floor when the thistle seed puffs in the corners had accumulated to tremulous quivering heaps. She and Stan sat together each evening. Elspeth was in bed by eight. They gave up the television. The picture, never the best because of the mountains, now lurched continuously, rolling them into its world of home life and splattered violence, its marvels of nature, sport, and innovative advertising.

— It's a good advertisement though, said Jinny one night before they flagged the whole thing away in disgust. They stared at a lavatory seat lid quacking between rolls. — You remember a talking lavatory seat.

Stan located his matches and relit his pipe. — You remember the talking seat he said. — Not the product. So it's not.

— Mmm said Jinny. She put out a hand, palm upwards in silent expectation of his box of matches.

The next day she nailed a loop of leather strap either side of the fireplace so she and Stan could hang their feet as they dozed, smoked or listened to The Weather. Shona and Fiona never discussed with Jinny what would happen, you know. Later.

Ellespie never had a knife. It hadn't seemed worth it though she learnt eventually. She continued reading and went North to Training College. The lines on her father's forehead creased in concentration when she showed him the letter. He snapped his glasses back in their case. — Why d'y'want to go up North? he said.

Ellespie felt as though she had been caught red-handed, the jam spoon dripping on the storeroom floor.

— Oh well she said. — You know Stan.

— Know what?

— See the world. All that.

He drove her to the bus in silence but that was nothing new.

———

Everything about it was good. The tugging wind trapped and cornered by buildings, steep short cuts bordered by Garden Escapes, precipitous gullies where throttling green creepers blanketed the trees beneath. And Bruno. Occasionally if she woke in the night when he'd yanked the duvet off her she thought of Stan, how he seemed impervious to heat or cold, an automaton programmed for work.

— My father doesn't trust town men she told Bruno one day. — Christ in concrete he yelled with delight. — Where've you been! It's like living with someone from the Lost City of Atlantis. She twisted the sludge coloured mug so the crack was on the other side. — I don't know about the Lost City of Atlantis she muttered. — I've got a book about it somewhere he said.

He had a book about everything. They lay in bed all Sundays reading, swapping occasionally. — Read this bit. — The man's a wanker. — Yeah but . . . His arms were beautiful hairy triangles to support his thrusting head.

— God I'm hungry he moaned. It was a test, a gamble. Who gave in first, who crawled groaning from the low bed to pull on something and grope to the dairy. She had seen Dustin Hoffman in *Kramer versus Kramer* zip his jeans like that. Not looking.

On Saturdays if they weren't reading or making love they went to the gym. They sweated with the righteous, each cocooned in her/his personal individualised workout programme. Self-absorbed as Narcissus they searched for themselves in ten foot mirrors, faces blank or contorted with loathing not love. They heaved and grunted, pulled and swung. Tab the flab. No gain without pain. Stan, Stan, it's me.

Bruno despised joggers. — Yon Cassius hath a lean and hungry look he roared. She looked it up in the Dictionary of Quotations under Cassius. — Give me men about me that have muscles! He seized her, squashing her nose against his Save the Whales. She loved him heart crutch mind and belly. He was a huge man, a towering hairy giant. His shape filled the doorway outlined in flame from the light in the hall as he groped to the bed and fell on her. — Where's the light. — It's shot she gasped. — Oh well I guess we'll make it. When she thought of Bruce and Doug, oh well never mind.

She wrote careful letters home. — A friend of mine Bevan and I went . . . Bevan, I call him Bruno, says . . . Jinny answered in her large looping scrawl. — Who's this Bevan/ Bruno? Stan wrote occasionally, painful lined one-pagers. — It's been hosing down since Mon. But we need the feed. How are your studies? All the best. Dad.

They were discussing abortion in the abstract when the telephone rang.

— I don't approve of it said Bruno, slipping a new insole into his gym shoe.

— You don't what? she said.

— I said I don't . . . He stood up. — O.K., O.K. I'm coming he snarled. He clumped to the telephone hobbling on one shoe and lifted the receiver.

— Yeah. Yeah she's here. Hang on. He turned and waved the receiver vaguely in the air.

Ellespie slid along the dinette seat. — Who is it?

— Didn't say. He handed her the receiver and plonked down again to concentrate on his insole, smoothing it in place with careful splayed fingers.

— Ellie here.

— Ellespie? The voice was faint. The line bad.

— Jinny! Toll calls, like kisses, were for crises. — What is it? she said.

— Dad. He rolled the truck.

— Is he all right?

— He's dead, the flat voice answered.

— Jinny! gasped Ellespie. Bruno's head lifted. — I'll come straight away she said.

— You don't have to. Not straight away. Shona and Fif. They're . . .
— I'll come tonight.
— O.K. Thanks.
— Jinny?
— Yes.
— How are you?
— I'll meet the plane then, said Jinny. — Unless I hear.

Jinny picked her up at five o'clock. The foothills were unattainable golden lands, the mountains hidden by cloud. The Airport was a paddock equipped with aeronautical essentials. It's air of makeshift impermanence was enhanced by the knowledge that the slab-like hut (office, lounge, conveniences) was opened only once a day for the arrival of this plane. As she came down the steps Ellespie saw Jinny scowling into the sun, hands thrust deep in her pockets. She didn't move to meet Ellespie, kissed her, but avoided her sweeping hug. She picked up her sister's small pack and they marched meshed in silence to the car. This is totally one hundred per cent insane thought Ellespie. — Tell me about it Jinny she said a few minutes later as the Holden swung onto the farm road.

So Jinny told her. How he needn't have gone to town on Tuesday. Not really. There was nothing vital. Where it happened. That turn by Berenson's woolshed I'll show you. How Stan climbed out, he must have thought he was all right. I mean he stopped Ivan in the paper car, told him about the rolling. Ivan had seen the truck anyway, recognised it of course, checked it was empty. Dad had seemed O.K. Ivan said. He died ten minutes later. Ivan had been very decent. Everyone had. Rushing over with food. There had been a postmortem and all that. A haemorrhage of the brain. It can happen like that sometimes they said. Jinny's voice drained on, her eyes pulled straight ahead.
— And how's Mum?

The eyes flicked at her for a second.
— Just the same.
— But does she . . . ?
— It's hard to know.
— Jinny does she know he's dead?
— Oh yes said Jinny. — She knows he's dead. She sits with him.

— I have all the arrangements in train Jinny said later, her mouth grimacing to emphasise the euphemism. — Guess what the undertaker said! Her laughter was a crow of delight. Ellespie shook her head in silence.
— He squeezed my hand said Jinny, and said he regretted we had to meet in such tragic circumstances! God in heaven! Do you reckon they do a course?

She told Ellespie that they would have the morning together before Shona, Fiona and husbands appeared, having made child minding arrangements. But her room was empty when Ellespie opened the door early next day.
Ellespie sat with her mother who seemed pleased to see her and asked after her children. — I've always liked the Air Force she said. — There was a camp near us at home. Absolute charmers. Yes. She sat serene and vacant, even her knitting fingers stilled. — Have you seen your Father she said suddenly. — Yes said Ellespie.

She made macaroni cheese hoping she remembered correctly that it was Jinny's favourite not Stan's. She removed his towelling hat from the top of the fridge and hid it in the woolshed behind the pine logs, then corrected this absurdity and put it back.
The coffin rested on small trestles. It stood in the closed-in sunporch beside the lumpy divan, level with the Indian cotton curtains she had run up last time. Ellespie gazed at the effigy of her father which lay cushioned in white satin.

51

The skin was dragged tight over the beak nose, mounded eyelids sealed the eyes. Ellespie stared at the face against the shiny stuff and thought of Jinny.

At twelve thirty she went into the living room. Her mother was sunk in the rioting flowers of the sofa, her hands folded over the Journal of Agriculture open on her knees at Poultry Notes. Ellespie touched one of the still hands. — I'll be back soon Mum she said. I'm going to find Jinny. Her mother's sandy eyelashes blinked. — What's for lunch? she said.

Tracks fanned out from the back door. To the sheds, the vegetable garden, the hens, the garage. Jinny's old roan was tethered to the fence by the concrete shed, his head hanging. Ellespie ran across the paddock and fell in the door. Jinny was leaning against the wall smoking a cigarette.

— Hi she said.

Ellespie's shoes scuffed the concrete as she moved to her.

Relaxed, indolent, Jinny flicked the butt down the stump and heaved herself upright. She shrugged, the slightest lift of the shoulders. — Oh well.

At the door she turned to Ellespie.

— Come on, she said.

One Potato Two Potato

Nancy and Helen spend the summer in each other's pockets.
Helen's grandmother tells them so. Long bleached days pile
up behind them, flat as the town in which they live. An
Irish colleen, Nancy's father calls her, stamping the foot-
operated automatic pressing machine — press, phouugh,
suck, clang — PRESS. Nancy hears it sometimes in her
dreams, a lullaby for a motherless child, another of her
father's endearments. He sings Nancy with the laughing
face though this is sometimes muddled with Jeannie with
the light brown hair. He owns the only dry cleaning shop
in the town. A dusty lancewood slants in the window, a
river of sweat clamps the shirt to his back. Helen's mother,
Mrs Ellison, is clean and thus a good customer for things
she can't wash. — You'll tell me, Mr Davenport won't you?
Promise you'll tell me when I reach the stage of throwing
food down my front? Mr Davenport stares and promises.

He likes Mrs Ellison. All his ideas of a fine woman are
melded and joined in her contoured form. She doesn't flop
about in the heat like some of them. In fact she gives up
scanties in the hottest weather but who's to know. She
seems so certain so real. In a sense she comforts him for
the nervousness he feels about his inability to remember

his dead wife Kath. Well he *remembers* her of course but somehow . . . He shuts his eyes and sees her small head sunk in the pillow. Hears her voice calling. Don. Don. But it all went on too long. He can't remember her clearly enough before then, not when she was well that is, laughing, running even. It worries him. He feels cheated and watches Nancy with particular care as she leaps through life. — That's my girl he cries at the Main School Athletic Sports. — Have a go then Nance! And Nancy wins always, legs flashing, black curls damp on her forehead as she snatches the lime-green bottle from Helen's hand at the finishing line. — Don't drink it Nancee it's sou-er, warns Helen, but Nancy loves the stuff, flinging it down her throat till she chokes, wiping the back of her hand across her mouth like a boy.

They have known each other since Nancy slithered her bottom around the vinyl floor of the shop. Later they played together, dressing and undressing blank-faced dolls and avoiding Mr Davenport's feet. If he could see his way clear he would press the crumpled scraps of garments. Their eyes level with the clamping press, Nancy and Helen waited. — But Dad it's . . . — That's it Nance. It was better than nothing, they could see that, but the doubt remained.

Dolls fade; bikes increase the girls' range. Nancy skims back and forwards across the town to play at the Ellisons. She is welcome as Helen is an only.

Mrs Ellison's face wilts at home. The effort of keeping things nice is unremitting. Clothes flap on the line in segregated precision, a stray sock tossing among the skirts is re-pegged where it belongs. As soon as the clothes are dry Mrs Ellison snatches them from the line, flaps them slaps them till they lie subjugated and flat in the basket, all billowing flight extinguished. Sighing, Mrs Ellison heaves the cane basket up the back steps and begins damping. She sprinkles water from her hand, flipping the parched clothes in endless baptisms from an enamel font. Then she irons.

Mr Ellison is rarely visible. Occasionally if Nancy stays

late she hears him enter the front door, hears his fluting call. — I'm home. Mrs Ellison says nothing. She stamps the iron at the board. Her husband walks into the kitchen, stroking black strands of hair across his scalp.

    — Oh there you are.

    — Where did you think I'd be?

    —I think I'd better be off Mrs Ellison.

    — Right Nancy.

And Nancy leaps to her bike and pedals home so fast the pedals spin from beneath her feet. — Dad Dad I'm home! She buries her head in his hairy beautiful neck. — Give us a chance matey he says, moving the beer to his other hand.

Mrs Ellison's mother, Marjorie, often sits with her daughter during the ironing. She sits upright on the kitchen stool, hands attentive in her lap, her feet encased in navy shoes which mould themselves to her bunions. Occasionally she sags then slaps herself upright again. Her own husband died in his prime, far too young, carried away by incompetence at the hospital. A photograph in the lounge shows a man like a tree trunk holding a blurred Helen. Helen is apprehensive of her grandmother. — Shut your mouth child. Breathe through your nose. And Helen tries, snorting through her blocked nose till she bursts and she and Nancy fall about in helpless delight. — There's no call for that says Marjorie, but this is worse and Helen and Nancy rush out the back, bare feet scudding. Mrs Ellison still irons. Marjorie hitches up her skirt, stretches out her legs, peers at them then smooths her skirt down again. She picks a green thread between thumb and forefinger, rolls it into a tiny ball and drops it surreptitiously onto the floor. It doesn't show.

    — They tell me you've moved him out she says.

Mrs Ellison licks her fingers and flicks the iron. The spit hisses to nothing.

    — Who told you that she says.

— I heard.

— It's all over town too I suppose that he snores so hard
I can't get a minute's sleep. Her face is hot, her hands busy.

— Your father snored.

— Not like him.

— Worse.

— Never.

Newly ironed clothes have the cleanest smell in the world.
There is no sound but the hissing sweep of the iron.

— Moved him out snorts Marjorie.

Mrs Ellison snaps off the iron. — He's got a lovely room,
all redecorated you want to see it? Her mother is on her
feet jerking her skirt into position. She gives herself a little
shake. — Yes, she says. The progress upstairs is followed
by Nancy and Helen who have trailed in for a drink from
the tap. There is silence as they climb the figured carpet
except for the murmured skipping chant Nancy has on the
brain. One potato two potato three potato four.

— Mine's done up too says Mrs Ellison. She flings open
the door of the master bedroom, a large room filled with
light. Nancy has not seen this room before and is pleased
with the dressing table set on long spindly legs, its top
covered with bottles which scatter the light. Nancy fingers
one. Helen concentrates on trying to breathe through her
nose. Her grandmother is silent, registering the fact that
there is now only one single bed in the room. Its bedspread
is quilted birds, its eiderdown restuffed and puffed. — Never
in all my days says Marjorie.

Now Mrs Ellison is showing a smaller room. Her husband's
fly-tying equipment is neatly arranged on a small table. A
miniature vice holds the hook of a Hammill's Killer. The
body is formed from red wool twisted and tied with yellow,
the side feathers are grey partridge dyed green, tied in killer
fashion, a fluff of black squirrel fur for the tail lies beside
the vice. Hairy Dogs, Red Setters, Mrs Simpsons, Grey
Rabbits and other flies are arranged in boxes made for the
purpose which lie behind the vice. Mr Ellison is one of the

best amateur fly-tiers in the district and his creations are much in demand and sworn by. Helen likes to watch him working but Nancy finds it boring and Mr Ellison finds Nancy a Fidgety Phil. Mr Ellison's knobbled fingers weave and poke, his sharp-pointed scissors snip at the exact spot, strands of appropriately coloured wool hang around his bent neck. He whistles 'If I had a rose from you/For every time you made me blue/I'd have a room full of roses', and is happy. A cigarette lighter in the form of a miniature Toyota car sits alongside his ashtray. You press the wheel and flame spurts from the bonnet but Nancy has seen this before. Mr Ellison's sister brought it back from Japan. It is unexpected on several counts.

The room is refurbished with red curtains slashed with brown. A disintegrating cane chair piled with floppy cushions sits in front of the table. — He won't let me get *rid* of the thing says Mrs Ellison, giving Mr Ellison's string-binding job on the back leg a nudge with her open-toed sandal. It does mar the decor but Marjorie is not interested.

— Your father would never she says. — Outside girls, says Mrs Ellison and Nancy and Helen are glad to.

— One potato two potato three potato FOUR. Five potato six potato seven potato MORE!

Mrs Ellison and her mother return to the kitchen. Marjorie would like a cup of tea but Mrs Ellison is still smarting. She resumes the ironing in silence.

— Do you blind bake your Rough Puff? asks Marjorie.

Mrs Ellison glances up from Nancy's summer gym.

— For the bottom you mean?

— Yes.

Mrs Ellison gives the gym a quick shake and hangs it on a hanger on the back of the door. — Always, she says firmly. — Don't you?

But Marjorie is not caught out. — Oh yes, she says. — I don't know about this new stuff though. It sogs whatever.

— I never have any problem, says Mrs Ellison.

Marjorie gives in. — How about a cup of tea? she says. Mrs Ellison glances up from a pink towel in simulated surprise. — Oh if you *want* one she says.

— I'll make it. Marjorie knows her own mind. — Where are the afghans? she says.

— In the cupboard.

The eager hiss of steam continues.

One of the reasons Helen is apprehensive of her grandmother is that she must see her almost every day. She is taking piano and bikes around to practice on the upright Bentley in the front room of the box-like house where Marjorie lives alone. Family wedding groups line the walls, women stand sheathed like arum lilies beside large men. In one of the photographs Helen is a flowergirl. She is not a success. Her mouth hangs open and she gazes at her posy as though it might explode. Helen senses that her grandmother wants something from her but she is unable to work out what and this makes her nervous. One of Marjorie's treasures is her collection of old seventy-eights. Bing Crosby oozes and warbles through the still house. 'I'm dreaming of a white christmas' he confides. Marjorie is adamant. — They don't make music like that now she tells Helen.

Helen swoops her bike around the corner of the house and finds her grandmother sitting on the back porch drying her hair. It is long and falls over her shoulders in streams. — You look like a princess, Gran! — Rapunzel, Rapunzel let down your golden hair but yours is silver she says, pleased to find life imitating books. Her grandmother stares up at the skinny child, her speckled hand touches Helen's face for a moment. Then she stamps herself upright and twists her hair into a french roll. Her hands move deftly right left one two; the pins stab in. — It's dry now she says.

Mrs Ellison has organized a cottage at the beach. Helen's hands are twisted in supplication. — Please. Can't she come Mum?

Mrs Ellison is bland, — I'm very happy to have Nancy at any time you know that.

— Well? Helen shuts her mouth, breathless with hope.

— What if Mr Davenport asked you to stay at Turangi again? You said you were homesick.

Helen is silent for a moment but desperation drives. — I needn't go.

Her mother stares. — What would you say? How would you get out of it she asks.

The Turangi experience resurfaces. Helen sees herself as though she is circling above the scene like the blowfly which droned around the centre light each night as she snivelled into her lumpy pillow — homesick for what?

Mr Davenport went to the pub while Helen and Nancy read comics in the Holden. He brought drinks out for them, laughing and teasing his girls as they snatched at the dripping cans. Once a mate took the orders, a smiling man with a good solid gut beneath his T-shirt. He yelled across the vast car park to Mr Davenport who cupped a hand to his ear in exaggerated concern for clarity. — Fanta for a pretty girl and a *what*?

There was something about the place, felt in the air, trapped in the cobwebby corners of the bach. When Mr Davenport looked at her like that. When Nancy climbed into his bed in the icy mornings and she hung back. Come on Hen, he said, it'd freeze a brass monkey out there, hop in. But Helen remained shuffling her bare feet on the coir matting. She watched Mr Davenport scratching the exuberant black hair which sprouted from the neck of his striped pyjamas. He stared at her. His voice was gentle. — You'll swallow a fly one day Hen you know that?

— I want to go home mumbled Helen.

— All right Mum.

Mrs Ellison smiles. How about the girl Barwick she says.
— No.

Helen thinks of Nancy. Of how she runs. Sees her hair always in a mess, snagged and tangled at the Baths after lengths. Sees her outside the Aztec Milk Bar that very day as she steps across the gutter to the footpath, a dancing movement, toe turned out like Miss Stringer at Ballet, not that either of them go. Nancy wouldn't be seen dead.

Nancy is still in Helen's mind as she skids her bike to a halt at the Ellison's back door after practice. Mr Davenport is standing close to her mother. He jumps, snatches a handkerchief from his pocket and scrubs his face. — Deliveries, deliveries, he mutters through the blue Eskay.

— Nancy told me you'd dropped deliveries. Helen is positive. — As from last month. She told me.

Mr Davenport is delighted. He laughs loudly. — Well there you go. Just a few specials.

Mrs Ellison is also laughing. — How many she says.

Mr Davenport flings his arms in the air with joy just like Nancy. He is panting with shared laughter. — Wouldn't you know eh wouldn't you know. He hugs Helen. — You'll do me he says. He riffles her hair then turns and runs around the corner still laughing.

Mrs Ellison's laughter stops. — Oh well she says and moves to the stove.

One potato two potato three potato *FOUR*. Helen has got it on the brain now.

The telephone rings trilling down the hall as Helen comes in from practice next day. She lifts the receiver and stands silent as a man's voice breathes at her.
— Is your Mum there?

Helen clutches the receiver tightly.
— No, she lies.

She listens with her shoulders hunched as Mr Davenport's words stream on. Her hand moves to the back of her neck.
— No, she says. — No. Don't. She drops the receiver back

and runs into the kitchen. Her Mother is poking the joint. She slams the oven door shut and straightens up with the skewer clenched upright in her hand.

— Who was it? she says.

— Wrong number. Helen knows the lie is hopeless. She scents defeat, sees Nancy leaping away. Mrs Ellison drops the skewer in the sink and turns to her daughter. — Helen? she says. It is a statement of intent. The light from the dying sun is blinding. Helen moves slightly.

— A man, she says.

— What did he want?

— Sexual intercourse, says Helen. — On the telephone.

— On the telephone! Mrs Ellison throws back her head and laughs. Helen's legs are heavy, her arms hang. She stares unhappily at the strong cords of her mother's outstretched neck.

Mrs Ellison is still laughing. She laughs and laughs and laughs. Tears spurt from her eyes. She flops onto the kitchen stool and wipes her eyes with the patchwork oven mitt. Helen's mouth hangs open, her eyes are on her mother's face. She is saved.

— Oh my God gasps Mrs Ellison. — On the telephone.

Egypt is a Timeless Land

The young man beside her was determined she should see them. He seized her hand and pointed it at the window as though this would achieve contact.

— See? he said. — See? Look. There! He was almost prostrate in her lap as he leaned across, willing her to see, insisting with force that she didn't miss the pyramids. The hair in his ear was soft and downy. His face was solemn with the intensity of his commitment.

— You're not looking he said, his face a foot from hers.

— I am!

— Well?

She squinted past her husband in the window seat.

— There, do you mean?

— No!

Peter's eyes lifted from *War and Peace*. He always read it on long air trips. Invaluable. Time flies, he told people. He smiled at the young man. — Give it up, he advised.

There was something far below on the brown flatness. A sort of geometrical smudge, two or more.

— I see them, she cried. — There!

— Yes!

Sheila and the young man Grant (in computers, business trip) leaned back and smiled at each other with relief.

— Thank you, she said. — I'd never have spotted them.

— Oh well, said Grant. — That's O.K.

She put her hand on the hefty thigh stretching the trouser fabric beside her. He glanced at her then moved the leg slightly. She was staring straight ahead at the back of the seat in front of her.

Grant seized his other ankle with both hands and jerked the knee to his chin several times, then repeated the process with the leg from which she snatched her hand. — Pity to miss them, he said, pausing for a moment to reassure the face beside him.

— While they're there, said Peter from the battle of Borodino. He glanced across at Grant as though seeing him for the first time in ten thousand miles. — Did you see that a bit fell off the Sphinx? he said.

Grant leant forward in excitement. — Now? he gasped.

Peter shook his head and picked up his book. — Months ago, he said. — Huge. Four hundred tonnes. You'd better be quick.

Grant looked at him warily. There was no response. Sheila smiled. Grant continued his in-flight exercises, his face tense with the concentration of one who knows he is on to a good thing.

Peter yawned hugely and shifted his buttocks.

The drinks trolley appeared from the pantry, clanking beneath the prepared face of an air hostess. — Thank God muttered Peter. Grant didn't drink but he could go a Coke.

Only the canteen staff trapped behind glass and carbohydrates seemed calm. The first-years sat on tables, their scarves discarded on the floor among spills and pieces of sodden bun. Someone screamed, the sound slicing the background din.

Peter pushed the debris to one side of a littered table and tore off his jacket. His striped cotton shirt was soft

and beautiful. He flopped onto the chair, rubbing his hands.
— Aah, he said, This is the life.

Sheila watched his jaws clamp the rubbery bun. The
unclamped bit parted like joke lips. Mock cream seeped out,
stained with crimson. — Junk, she said.

— I like it, he mumbled.

— You shouldn't!

— Try and stop me, he said, licking his fingers.

— O.K.

He pulled a grey handkerchief from the pocket of his
corduroys, slapped it against his mouth, then shoved it back.
His smile was wide, generous to her imperfections.

— You try too hard, he said touching her cheek with
one sticky finger.

She had come down to Dunedin at the beginning of the
year, virtually hand in hand with Tom Rallings. They had
been joint Head Prefects at High, led blameless academic
lives and opened the Leavers' Ball, clasped alone and together
on the empty floor for the first surge of the Leavers' Waltz.
Their parents were friends. Until Sheila's father died they
played euchre week by week in each others' cluttered houses.
Sheila and Tom knew they were lucky. Lucky to be clever,
lucky to have won Scholarships, lucky oh especially lucky
to have each other in their mothball-scented homeknits to
hug and confide in, and what would they have done if they
hadn't.

— Throw them *away*, for heaven's sake, said Jill, her first
roommate at the hostel.

— But what about the moths!

— Bugger the moths. Jill dropped lean and dangerous
onto her moccasin heels and began snatching the white balls
from among the woollens in the bottom drawer. — Four!
God, I'd rather have the holes anytime. She threw the things
down the lavatory where they melted to scented sludge.

Tom was residual, lingering from home, part of her
familiar knobbly past. When the sun shone his parents sat

side by side on a collapsing sofa on the front verandah acknowledging the world with a wave, a lifted hand.

— Yes, they replied. — Yes. Tom's away now, down south, getting his letters.

He was unable to get into a hostel and lodged with a bitch in London Street. The food was bad, his room pokey, but it had a desk and a view of a patch of grass. He watched the male blackbird and its mate, which he had always thought was a thrush until Zoology 1. He admired their ability to wait, head cocked sideways waiting for the strike. In the meantime he had Sheila.

They were both surprised when Peter Rossiter picked her from the pool. Tom was left, but not without resources. He found Jocelyn all by himself and life continued.

Sheila's mother was not pleased and told her so in the August break. — What have you got against Tom anyhow? — Aw Mum said Sheila, rubbing the chilblain on her heel. Do shut up and take that *thing* off your head why can't you, she thought, but that was how Mrs Greer did her hair, and very useful it was too, her Curl Tidy. She also had a Breeze Bonnet for the main street where the wind was a whetted knife. Sometimes Mrs Greer wore a navy blue beret with her blue and white striped jersey. She looked like a leery matelot. Sheila was an only daughter after two sons but by no means a gift. A challenge rather, as no woman can expect perfection in male offspring.

Peter won her. He squatted in front of the open fire on Uncle Harry's pouf, arms hugging his knees in *Boyhood of Raleigh* attentiveness to her recent widowhood. — When you're on your own with boys you know, it's not easy, said Mrs Greer. Her round face was belligerent as she stoked the fire, scrabbling and stabbing at its core.

— I'm sure you're right said Peter. He put out a hand for the poker. — I'll do it. She declined his offer. — They make a mess of it see. They just wiggle and the whole flaming thing falls through, she explained.

Peter leant forward. — I *see*, he nodded.

Mrs Greer gazed at his thoughtful face. A lock of hair fell across his forehead as he told her of his night shift job in a Dunedin bakery and his problems with the smalls.

— At that stage, four o'clock in the bloody morning, he said, just when I thought it was all over, he produced the smalls!

— The whats? said Mrs Greer.

— The smalls.

Too difficult. Mrs Greer begs for help, her face anxious. Loving the story, she wants it all. — What are the smalls? she insists.

Peter is on his feet demonstrating. He is dabbing icing on small cakes, slipping a stab of jam between puffs, a blob of mock cream deep in the throats of pastry cornucopias. Mrs Greer can just see his long arms stretching, his hair flopping, his floury hands. She loves him.

Sheila loves him later when he creeps down the icy hall past Mrs Greer's snores. — This place is like the South bloody Col, he mutters as she welcomes him onto her slumped wire-wove.

He liked Woodville. The shop verandahs which waited for shoot outs, the bar doors which swung. The decor of the Daisy Lee Milk Bar exceeded his hopes, though the Banana Split was a disappointment, as was Glenda's hairstyle. The classic style for Milk Bar ladies, he told Glenda (who was one tough lady according to Sheila's brother John) is piled high in front and hanging down at the back. Glenda didn't thump him. She touched her back hair and smiled. — Have you ever thought of Christchurch? asked Peter sprawling across the counter. But Glenda knew that one day her prince would come and so he did eventually. Terry Auburn from the Coast.

Sheila finished her degree. She had intended to do Diatetics but the money was better in teaching and they were saving. They married the week Peter qualified. The wedding was all right — well, all right. Peter's parents were divorced. His mother, a shy almost speechless woman, lived in Dunedin and came up nervously with Peter. Peter's father and his new wife Sandra flew up from Christchurch and had to be collected from Palmerston by a groomsman. Everyone did the best they could, though it did make the wedding photographs a bit lopsided as Sandra insisted. — I'm not *invisible* am I? she said adjusting the rake of her hat outside the church door.

The bride and groom sat at the top table flanked by the bridal party. Sheila leant forward reaching for an asparagus roll. — I'm having an asparagus roll, she told Peter. She turned to him quickly, her face half hidden by the stiff tulle. — Peter, she said. Have an asparagus roll. But his mouth was full of sausage and pastry and he couldn't even smile.

When Sheila won the Scholarship Miss Egerton tried to talk her out of Home Science. — I've nothing against Home Economics, she lied, shaking her puff of thin gold curls, but with your brain . . . You could go *on*. — You can go on in Home Economics, said Sheila. She had no intention of going on, other than to a perfect marriage and sublime motherhood, and Home Economics provided the best resource material available for working towards her goal.

They rented a derelict cottage in Mount Victoria. Sheila ran up curtains, she upholstered and resprung, she painted and transformed when she came home from school each day. She was like something out of an ancient request session, waving Peter farewell from her gingerbread trellis fence each morning, running to kiss him as he bounded up the steps from the money market each evening. They made love on the floor, the kitchen table, in the shower. They were inventive.

And then Simon made three and Sheila never worked again.

And the parties, oh the parties, and the candles and the fun. She could adapt any recipe. — It's my training she said modestly. Her guests relaxed, motoring through the *Terrine aux foies de volaille* (Yours? Yes. Ttt.) in the knowledge that Sheila would make them well fed and Peter would make them informed and cheerful for he was both and such attributes are transferable.

But she tried too hard.

— Fuck the Hollandaise! cried Peter when he found her tense and stiff-fingered, surrounded by empty eggshells and something yellow and curdled in a double boiler beside the baby's bottle.

— I can't serve the Haplens your bloody trout without Hollandaise, she said rounding on him, the wooden spoon raised.

— Why not? He knew he was on shaky ground.

— Because trout is the most tasteless fish in the whole bloody world and you catch it and I fight with it, she said slamming back to the stove.

He considered kissing the back of her neck but decided against it.

She rescued the sauce with an extra yolk.

— Delicious, murmured Donald Haplen, slipping the fork between pink lips. — Tell me Peter, he said after a pause for mastication. — What do you make of this positive discrimination?

— Oh essential, said Peter. Candlelight suited him. It emphasised the beak of his nose, the bones and hollows of his cheeks. — Essential, he repeated firmly.

— I don't agree at all, said Shona Wooton who had a mind like a man. She'd been told. She drank without favour from Peter's wine glass and her own. He made no comment, bending forward to obtain her permission each time he refilled the glasses. It was difficult to catch her eye. It returned to her glass accompanied by a pretty little flutter of surprise each time she found it replenished.

— The opportunities are there, she said, touching the corners of her mouth with a napkin. — Equal education. It's all *there*.

— When I was teaching at Mangere, said Sheila, who had something to say but was swept away to the hostess bin.

— But surely Peter, in your position, said Donald, his hand engulfing his wineglass, you must see the *results* of such insanity. Can't read, can't write, can't spell!

— Would you put all that down to positive discrimination? enquired Peter, pushing back his hair. Wise Peter, who is informed and keeps calm and is liberal.

And what about Viet*nam*? cries Joanna Haplen.

The babies, ah the babies. All she had hoped for and more. When Sheila thinks about that time, the years melt to a warm fecund haze of loving and being loved and being essential and minding and caring and knowing how lucky she was. Where was Peter? There, but cackhanded and useless really. Useless. She could do it in half the time and did, her body dipping and twisting to do up Simon, put down Vicki, change and feed Jack and love every minute of it as she should and did.

Peter read to them of course. His head formed the apex of a familial pyramid on the sofa; long father, small intent children, loved books. They tried the new words, testing for taste. Peter was amused when they preferred the meticulous detail of Giles' cartoons to the pale dreamy illustrations of the children's literature Sheila kept up with. He read aloud to each successive baby from his own reading, the infant cradled in the crook of his arm waving starfish hands; Dostoevsky occasionally, when he was giving the guy yet another final chance, but usually hefty paperbacks, in-depth biographies, or sagas at a sweep. The children amused him and he was pleased they seemed to be developing a sense of humour.

— I can do a joke, said Simon.

Peter, horizontal on the sofa, put down *American Caesar* with courteous attention.

— Great, he said. — Tell me.

— Ha ha ha, said Simon.

— Very funny, said Peter, picking up the open book. — Go and tell Mum.

His son stumped off. Peter heard his solemn Ha ha ha from the open plan kitchen of the new house, but the reply was inaudible.

— What's funny about this one, Dad? — Hang on, said Peter. He hunkered down onto the carpet beside Vicki and the discarded *New Yorker* from the office. A frizzle-faced woman was placing something equally frizzled on the plate of a disheartened looking man beside her. 'I think it's nature's way of telling me to stop cooking,' said the caption.

— It's rather difficult to explain, honey, said Peter. — The lady is tired of cooking.

— Why? said Vicki.

— Just sick of it, I guess. Not like Mum, said Peter, tickling his daughter till she squealed.

They went for picnics. Peter sat in the car and relayed the best bits of *The Goon Show* to Sheila as she ran in and out to the house with cartons for him to stow in the Datsun with meticulous care.

He assumed the horizontal as soon as possible on arrival, thankful to be at one remove from the sodding garden. Sheila stared at the wide sea. I am bossy. I do too much. He supports us all. I nag.

— Where's Jack!

— What? said Peter from beneath the decent sun hat so difficult to find.

— Jack! She was on her feet, leaping across the sand. — Jack!

Simon and Vicki glanced up from their industrious nimble-legged digging and watering, their togs minuscule and damp around their thighs.

— Here, said Vicki.

- We've buried him, said Simon.

Jack waved, an involuntary gesture. His infant smile was calm. He was covered to his nipples with damp sand.

The back of his neck beneath her nuzzling mouth was warm and pleated.

— My darling, my darling, my sweetest love, she muttered.

— I'm sorry. I'm sorry.

— For God's sake, said Peter, lifting the hat for a moment, what are you sorry about now?

She flung herself into everything connected with her dream. Play centre and PTA offered grist. She enjoyed being with people who cared, who were determined to fight, to accept nothing but the best, who gave their time, their effort and outrage to benefit their young. She became Chairperson of both. — Drunk with power, muttered Janet Mill after her defeat over the bus trip to Bushy Park. Of course it wasn't too far, and they must see the kakapo. — We have cars, Sheila explained to Janet who was angrily zipping up her padded windjacket, but a lot of parents haven't.

— Is that right? said Janet.

Simon and Vicki enjoyed Cubs and Brownies until the uniforms were bought and they got sick of it. Sheila spent her days leaping in and out of the car, stowing, fetching and carrying for endless lessons and activities they were good at and which must therefore be encouraged.

— Relax said Peter.

— You spoil them, said her mother. — Where's your own life? Let the little buggers go by bus. What are you?

— If they have the talent . . . Sheila knew she was right, armoured in unselfishness.

The children loved staying with Gran even though there wasn't an electric blanket in sight and the lavatory was freezing. Its walls had been painted blue and later pink and there were interesting patterns where the blue resurfaced.

Mrs Greer insisted they travelled to Woodville by bus, as though this would strengthen moral fibre. One at a time, as Gran wasn't the girl she used to be, my word. The

Manawatu Gorge with the river swirling below meant they were nearly there. The cliffs were tied back with wire to keep the rocks under control.

Gran fried bread and eggs and bacon and sausages and fritters and to hell with cholesterol which she was appalled to discover Jack knew about when he was six. — Don't forget the Daisy Lee, said Peter every time one of his offspring departed for a holiday with Gran. But it had gone long ago, turned into a video parlour which didn't last either.

Large uncles with homespun wives welcomed them on to the farms they managed and fed them home-killed mutton in warm kitchens. Uncle Frank's had a framed reproduction of Winston Churchill beneath a high hat, his face clamped around a cigar, two fingers signifying victory.

Where had it all gone? How had it happened?

Sheila insisted on meals together at the table. (— Sitting up like vultures. Vicki.)

— A meal is a social occasion, she told them, matching stubborn face to sullen.

— You try too hard, said Peter into her ear as he turned off the televison.

Simon, who was between flats, sat on a high stool in the kitchen picking at his bare feet. She looked at them in amazement, peels and snatches of yellow parchment of skin lay on the cork tiles, his big toes were double-jointed personnel.

— Simon!

He lifted his head. — Yeah?

— What on earth are you *doing*?

His smile was gentle but dangerous. — Picking my feet.

— Well stop.

— Why?

She seized a cloth and opened the oven door. — Because it's disgusting.

— Why?

— Oh shut up, said Sheila, slamming the casserole onto the heat resistant mat on the table. And clean up that mess.

— Some social occasion, yawned Vicki all over the coleslaw.

— Don't be rude to your mother, said Peter, touching his daughter's Pre-Raphaelite tangle of blond curls. He took the coleslaw from her hands, placed it on the table and patted the back of the chair beside him. She sank down and lifted her head to smile at him.

Sheila clung to Peter in bed at night as they lay beneath the duvet which was always too hot, whatever they said about stroking the feathers down to the bottom. — Why does he? When will they? Why don't they? she begged. — Relax said Peter. He stroked her till she obeyed, then rewarded her.

His tolerance was wide. He shared the odd roach with Simon as long as Simon aired the room. — Your mother wouldn't like it. His long tapered fingers stretched out to his son in supplication, his snorting laugh was infectious. They had the same taste in comedy and late late horror films, stretched side by side in comfort long after Sheila had huffed off to bed. Nothing shocked him, no joke went too far. Simon and Vicki liked him.

Jack was five years younger than Vicki. A child worried since infancy, his eyes, deep set and blue as Peter's, were troubled. His hair curled as tightly as Vicki's but the colour was a dusty brown. He had his mother's concern to lay hold on life, to get it right. They sat in companionable silence for hours as they drove up to see Mrs Greer who was warmer than she had ever been in her life in an overheated Rest Home in Dannevirke. They were at ease together. — Ma, he called her. — Ma, look at that.

She ran with quick scurrying steps from sofa to chair, snatching one unplumped cushion after another, slapping it into shape and repiling it in a confused harmony of apricot and strong pink against the back of the sofa.

She increased her Meals on Wheels to twice a week.

— How would you feel if I asked you to drive today? she said to Simon who was between jobs as well as flats this time. — Trapped, he said. — Do you have to have your hair tied up in knots like that? You look so *stuck*.

Sheila would never have asked Vicki, who passed every LL.B. exam with languid ease and treated her mother with the contempt she deserved.

— Why don't you do something *real*, Mum? she said one day when the washing machine in her flat had packed up.

— Real like what? said Sheila, clutching the protective colouration of the washing pile to her.

— Something *real*. Sexual Abuse Help Foundation say.

— I do!

— Just money. You're not on the roster.

— Look at me, cried Sheila, Would you want *me* to . . . ?

— You're just fluffing about, interrupted Vicki. — It's the same with Amnesty. You don't *do* anything.

— I give money. Collect.

— *Collect*. The scorn resurfaced. — You don't even read the magazine.

— I do.

— You burn it. I never see it. I didn't know it existed till the other day.

I will not tell you about the double amputees. I will not describe how the man described how he was blindfolded, given a sedative, how he heard one hand and one foot hit the ground at the same moment. I will not tell you how he said he still has nightmares. As though it could be otherwise and what help is it to the sedated that I'share them.

She shoved the washing into the hole and added the soap.

Vicki pressed the button.

Sheila's eyes itched unbearably. — I want to tear them out of my head, she told the hand-stitched lapels of the consultant's three piece suit. He rose quickly, the rounded

74

belly suddenly at eye level. — Come, he said. — Let me examine them.

— You have inadequate tears, insufficient oil in them to lubricate the eyeball. I will give you some drops, said the man, — which will alleviate the problem.

She worked up the story a little. She was always glad of non-controversial material, much of which showed her in a slightly ludicrous light. Simon and Vicki were not interested. Jack patted her arm and told her she could be Miss Inadequate Tears. His siblings groaned. Peter had missed it.

The dim little story trickled away but Jack remembered it. — Hi Inadequate, he greeted her as he crashed up the steps to dump his schoolbag at her feet. — There y'go, Inadequate.

He was more confident. The Seventh Form, he told her, was piss in the hand. He had always been a solitary child, sitting at the kitchen table while she cooked, making them cups of tea in a red pot, licking basins and wringing her with sad tales of rejection by peers which required bracing anecdotes of sticks and stones and ducklings and swans. Suddenly she was surrounded by hairy men in short pants who scarcely glanced at her as they loped through the kitchen shouting for Jack.

She was delighted. — Isn't it marvellous about Jack?

— Nnnn? said Peter. The leader was useless again. Rhubarb rhubarb and the summary tied up with pink ribbon. Pompous clown. He should write a letter. Dear Sir, With regard to your sewage outfall leader, with regard to your leader on sewage outfall . . .

— Jack. He's so happy.

— Good on him.

— I am tired, she told the family doctor, watching his fingers as they stroked the computer keyboard.

He swung round to give her the benefit of his full

attention. — Tired, he said. — That's no good.

— I have never been tired. Never. I can't decide things.

— What sort of things?

— Anything. Which vegetable. Which meat. Pathetic things.

— Do you sleep well.

— No.

He nodded and made a note on the pad supplied by Bayer. — And? he said.

— I feel all shivery. I forget things.

— What sort of things?

She never had liked him. — Everything, she said.

— Such as?

— I can't decide things, she told Peter.

— Join the club, he said.

She worked on it. She took more exercise, charging up the hill each day like a bee on heat. (Jack.) She considered the gym. She stopped the evening sherry and felt colder than ever.

She put a pad by the bed for essential things she might remember in the night and examined it in the morning.

'Potatoes,' she deciphered. 'Chocolate hail. Get up.' She flung the crumpled scrawl from her as though it was infected.

She ran around the gorse covered hills of Cairo in a dream. — I have lost my bag, all my papers, my passport, she told the three people who crouched in her brother Frank's cowshed. — Do not bother us, they said. — Which is the way to Cairo? she begged. — I have lost my bag. — That way, said one, pointing up the farm track. — No that way, said the tiny woman in stripes and an organdy collar. — I have lost my bag! she screamed.

Peter shot upright, his hand snatching for the light.

— God in heaven! He blinked at her through lank hair.

— You don't look too hot, What's up? He patted the

mattress. — Lie down. There, there, he said giving a quick
heave on the duvet before subsiding.

— What's the matter with me? she asked next time.
— Is this what they mean by nervous collapse?
   He laughed. — I haven't heard that expression for years.
   — Breakdown then?
   — Such upsets are common in women your age. Though
of course I'm no expert, said the smug child.
   — Why!
   — You are depressed.
   — How can I be depressed! Look at Jane Carson. (Tragedy,
real tragedy, death and bitter grief.) She's not *depressed*.
   — Mrs Carson is a very strong woman. There was silence
as they thought of Mrs Carson. He made another note.
— We'll get you an appointment with Nigel Braithwaite
as soon as possible. He leant back in his swivel chair, gave
a swirl in the direction of the door and stood up. — Medically,
he said, you are depressed.

— Nigel Braithwaite wants to see you as well, she told Peter.
   — Why? He looked up from the bed, his hand hidden
by a shoe.
   — I don't know.
   — O.K. He leant forward and tugged at the laces.
   — When? he said, his voice muffled.

They sat side by side in the cramped waiting room. Peter
picked up a magazine. — Not many places have *Punch* now,
he said. — Too bloody Brit.
   They all looked quite sane. An older man. Two women,
one plus Sheila. The younger woman lay slumped beside
a pallid child with breathing problems. The toes of the
mother's track shoes turned up like a blunted jester's. White
sheep trekked across her red jersey. The child sucked its
thumb, the mother yanked it out without a glance. The

child sucked its thumb. The process was repeated. They waited.

The psychiatrist sat miles away scribbling in longhand on a large pad. Sheila kept hefting her chair closer. There were no pictures.

— How can she be depressed if she says she's not depressed? asked Peter. — She's not a fool.

He didn't answer. He kept asking about her parents.

— I can't decide things. I'm cold.

— Sheila's always been such a competent person, said Peter.

Nigel Braithwaite explained about the pills. — Don't worry if they leave a dry taste, a dry *feel* rather. In the mouth.

They picked them up from the local chemist on the way home.

The pills were marvellous. The improvement astonishing.

She was making Hummus for Peter's birthday. ('This well known chick pea dip for nibbling, especially with warm pita bread.')

Peter folded the paper to the entertainment page. — Aah, he said.

— What?

— Nothing. He put down the paper, reaching for his pocket diary and consulted a page. — Ah, he said. — Good. He glanced at his thin oblong watch. — Would you like a drink?

Her face was anxious, her lips pursed above her licked finger. — It always takes more lemon than they say, she said.

He paused on his way to the cupboard. — What?

— Nothing. He lifted the sherry bottle. She shook her head. — No, not with those pill things.

Hummus, Lamb with prunes and apricots, Spicy lentils with zucchini, Eggplant salad, Spinach salad with yoghurt and Coriander bean balls for the feast. 'These interesting little morsels are very tasy although a little messy to hold, so make sure you have plenty of paper serviettes to hand. They can be prepared a day in advance. Do grind your own coriander seeds for this recipe (in a coffee grinder or similar), as the intoxicating fragrance of coriander quickly dissipates.' She rolled another little morsel between her fingers then dipped them in lemon juice as recommended.

Next day she reread the recipe for Lamb with apricots and prunes. It sounded disgusting. Why on earth had she . . . The Eggplant salad was easy, the Spicy lentils with zucchini had better be good. She dried her hands and reached for the next recipe, Spinach salad with yoghurt. She opened the refrigerator and scrabbled in the hydrator. Nothing. Her hands panicked. She backed out and slammed the door. Sheila is such a competent person. She seized her parka from its hook by the back door, grabbed her change purse and keys and skittered down the steps to the garage. Just accept it. Don't fuss. Everyone forgets.

She stood in front of the racks of vegetables which were still sparkling from Bob's sprinkler. The spinach was five dollars seventy a kilo. But the silver beet might be too coarse. Competent. Competent. The drops of water were beads of silver, meeting, running together, dripping as she stared. There was a puddle on the floor beneath the broccoli. She began swaying very slightly from side to side, her hands clenched around her purse, the keys at her wrist on a wooden bead bracelet. She was shaking, her lips clamped together as she moved from one shelf to another feeling her way to the door. Bob glanced at her, his bald head shiny beneath the flickering miniature TV on the wall. — You O.K. then, Mrs Rossiter.

They were very kind. Jay took her hand, led her out the back and sat her on a hard chair by a large sink full of spinach. He made a cup of tea. The medallion from his last visit to India swung forward on its gold chain as he handed

79

her the mug. — Just take it quietly, he said. There were
discarded lettuce leaves on the floor, over-ripe fruit in boxes,
a single light. — Thank you, Jay, she said. How old are
you?

Twenty two. His teeth were perfect. — I'll ring Mr
Rossiter? What's the number?

— Number?

— For his office.

— Why?

— Once he hears we've got you in the back room he'll
be up like a rocket.

She smiled, her hands balled against her chest with the
effort of remembering — Seven double six two five seven.

He stood at the telephone beside her, his arms smooth
and brown. She clutched herself and began rocking
backwards and forwards in a steady rhythm. Jay glanced
at her and nodded his head. — O.K. thanks, he said and
put down the receiver.

— He's not in the office.

— Why?

— They don't know.

— They must know.

— He's not there. His face was unhappy, the skin beneath
his eyes looked bruised. — I'll run you home in the truck.
No sweat.

Something was ringing in her head. — I've got the car.
There's nothing wrong with me.

— Come on then, he said. — No sweat.

Peter sat in still contentment as the lights came up and
the audience, mostly matinée loners, drifted out. What a
man, he thought. A oncer. A genius. A birthday treat. Sheila
had never liked him, she thought him heartbreaking. And
two more to come. A Chaplin festival, dumped midweek
at the Paramount. He stretched, heaved himself upright in
the murky light and groped his way out, side-stepping the

queues for the next session. And there had been virtually no publicity.

The bus was full. The driver seemed enraged, lurching and crashing to a vicious stop at the red lights, hurling his standing cargo backwards at the green. The squat little woman beside Peter lost her balance and clutched his arm. — Pardon me, she muttered, her eyes milky blue beneath her knitted tea cosy hat. Peter smiled. He felt tempted to tell her it was his birthday, that he'd just seen a marvellous film. — Dirty bastard, she snarled at Peter's chest, nodding her head in the direction of the driver's back. — He'll be old soon. Then he'll know eh. Peter's smiled widened. She reminded him of Mrs Greer; her gallant rage, her uncertain stance, her woolly hat. At the next stop she clung harder than ever until the bus stopped, then edged her way down the giant steps. The hat bobbed, she lifted a tiny pink hand in salute. — Taa, she said. Peter waved, hanging on with one hand for safety.

It was dark as he walked up the street. One or two fires were lit, the smoke ascending straight to heaven in the still air. The concrete steps to the porch were steep, the white paint on their edges worn. He must try and con Simon into repainting them. His mind flicked to the film. He saw the genteel gestures, the fastidious finger sprinkling imaginary salt at the imaginary feast. He put down his briefcase, steadied it between his legs, dragged out his key and opened the door.

— Hul*lo* he called into the silence. He strolled into the kitchen and glanced around the mess of Middle Eastern feast preparation. — Hullo he called again.

She was sitting on the sofa in the dark.

— Hullo, she said.

Peter suggested the trip two months later.

Sheila turned off the toaster and dug out the slice with a knife.

— Why? she said. She plonked the toast on Peter's plate and sat down.

He bowed his head in thanks. Because I went to the flicks.

— *Why* have you never liked Chaplin? he said munching.

She leapt from the table. He was on his feet, the toast in one hand, his mouth bulging. He clamped her wrist with his other hand and shoved her against the bench.

— O.K. I didn't know you were so ill. *Talk* about it for God's sake. I went to the *flicks*!

She moved her head. — You're spitting toast.

— Sweet Christ, he shouted. — Table manners! You've got a table manners mind.

— Yes, she screamed. — Yes. I have!

But he came back to it. He had to do something. He came home with travel brochures, photographs of bright delights in flat folders. — It's a good time, he said. — The dollar won't stay at this rate.

— I don't want to, thanks, she said. — I'm not being, you know, I just don't . . .

He took her hand and examined it as though it was something interesting, stroking a ridged vein back towards the wrist with the forefinger of his other hand.

— Give it a go, he said. — What about Egypt?

She picked up her mending. (Women don't *mend* now. Vicki.) She bit off a length of cotton with the quick snipping movement of her teeth which always jarred him, then threaded the needle, holding it up to the light, squinting through her bifocals at the minute hole.

— Egypt? she said, stabbing the needle at a black shirt which had lost a button.

Her father had rolled in from the pub singing his party song. It was years before she discovered it was a hymn.

There is a happy land
Far far away.

82

Where saints in glory stand
In bright array.

The rollicking sound echoed down the hall to her bedroom where she lay in bed with tonsillitis clutching a decadent hot water bottle. He clattered into the room in his work boots and flopped on her bed. He dumped a book on the eiderdown, narrowly missing the remains of her bread and milk. — There you are sweetheart, he said, botching an attempt to kiss her forehead and landing in her hair. — Bought you a present. He belched. — Because you're my little sweetheart that's why.

Not birthday, not Christmas, because she was his sweetheart he had bought her this beautiful book, *The Bible designed to be read as Literature*. Muddy black and white photographs of the Holy Lands and Egypt were distributed amongst the text.

'Egypt,' said the introduction, 'is a timeless land. These photographs were taken in the Twentieth Century but the scenes and scenery are unchanged since Biblical Times. The river and bullrushes are identical to those where Pharaoh's daughter and her handmaidens found the infant Moses. Methods of agriculture have not changed over thousands of years.' Camels plodded, water wheels turned, oxen pulled. The pyramids were not mentioned.

Her mother snatched the book and banged it against her apron as though beating dust from it. She glared at Sheila. — You know where he'll have got it don't you? she said. (She always called him He.) — The pub, that's where. It'll have fallen off the back of some bloody truck and he's been taken for a sucker again. Oh! The sound was a guttural explosion of disgust. — Designed to be read as literature my oath.

— Mum, whispered Sheila, her hand outstretched. — Let's have it, Mum.

83

— Yes, said Sheila, her hands hidden in the folds of the shirt. — Yes. I'd love to go to Egypt.

Peter even made the travel arrangements. He consulted Sheila, treating her wishes with consideration. He spoke a lot about the travel agent Sharyl: her competence, her knowledge, her huge earrings. They took the ten-day package with optional extras. — We'll see how we go, said Peter.

The plane landed into dry baking heat and confusion. They waved farewell to Grant across the seething terminal and eventually found a taxi. It hurtled through the streaming, screaming streets at high speed, the driver's hand hard down on the horn. Sheila assumed he knew what he was doing. — Look! Aren't they beautiful, she said pointing to two heroic figures in djellabas striding through the dust. — Why are there no fezzes?

— They went out after Farouk, said Peter, clinging to the seat. He preferred driving.

— Why?

— I'll tell you later, said Peter who was concentrating.

She leant back against him. — I should've read more of the modern stuff, she said.

The hotel had seen better days, an expression which pleased Peter. Sheila looked at the wide wardrobe which touched the ceiling, the enormous bed beneath the used-looking cover. — You get in first, she said. — In case something's died in the bottom. She put her arms around him and rubbed her head against his shoulder.

They were woken at four forty-five by the call of the Muezzin. They were right. It is haunting. She lay staring at the grey slit of sky. Come all to church good people, good people come and pray, to another God. The sound was plangent, hanging in the silence after the call had ceased. Peter shambled out of bed to the bathroom and walked

84

straight into the plate glass door with numbing force.

They sat at a window in the dining room eating croissants and sipping café au lait. The hotel lay on a tributary of the Nile. She watched a man far below in a small felucca. He stood at the stern and flung out a fishing net as in the photograph captioned 'I will make you fishers of men.' The net sailed out, settled a moment on the brown water, then sank. Life designed to be read as literature.

— Look. She showed Peter. — I've seen that before.

— Good coffee, said Peter, glancing around for refills. He smiled at her. — Where?

— I had a book. She had never told him about her father.

— Ah.

— It is timeless, she said, lifting her head to glance around the room. — There's Grant. She raised her coffee cup in greeting.

Grant, spruce and breakfasted and ready for the next flight, marched to their table.

— Coffee? smiled Sheila. Grant shook his head. Peter was still looking for more.

— How did you sleep? asked Sheila.

— O.K. said Grant, sitting down beside Sheila once more in his tight trousers. — I could've done without the whatever at five a.m. He had one finger between the pages of a paper back. — I've been reading, he confided. — My God, their religion was pretty weird. You know they thought they had to take everything with them? Whatever they'd need, want even. Did you know that?

— Yes, said Sheila.

— It says here . . .

— Ah thanks. Peter held out his cup to the crisp waiter bearing a silver-plated coffee jug. Sheila shook her head.

— It says here, said Grant, laying the book flat on the table, that they found an entire huge room full of mummified cats, each in its own little casket-type thing so that they could you know . . .

— Have one to hand? smiled Peter.

85

— Yeah, said Grant. He shuddered. — A room full of mummified cats for Christ's sake.

Sheila's fingers gripped the table. — But why shouldn't they? Her voice was high. — They might want a cat, she insisted. — You don't know! They might need one. Why shouldn't they have a cat? she demanded, staring at the scrubbed, startled face.

Peter put down his cup quickly and turned to stare out the window.

The man in the felucca had hauled the net in from his last cast. Although he was far below, Peter could see the thin body tense as he gathered the net once more, then flung it in a wide sweeping arc out across the water.

Commitment

David is obsessed by sex. Terri is not obsessed by sex, nor indeed by anything. She wishes to be obsessed by something. Committed. She wishes to stand up and be counted because commitment is all and she is not committed and bugger it.

Terri drains her coffee mug and replaces it on the Berber in our living room. She leans back defiant and uncommitted in the bean chair. She hits the chair angrily with the flat of her hand but the beans have nowhere to go. Terri's beauty is angular, she moves well, each action flowing from the one before. Her legs arrange themselves with grace, the angles sharp, flat kneecaps obvious beneath flesh smooth and brown as an egg. Her hair is black and hangs forward but she can flick it back in one sweeping swing and does so. Now she hooks a strand behind her right ear and glares at me.

— You're not committed she says.

In fact I am. Totally. So recently it is still contained.

She changes tack slightly. — It's because women have been brought up to please she says.

— Balls. I stand up, not sinuously. I roll out of my bean chair onto my knees and more or less take it from there.

Once upright I head for the divider of the open plan kitchen. I slam a teaspoon of Greggs in each mug and fill it from the saucepan on the stove because the kettle is still waiting to be picked up. I watch the boiling water swirl the instant into brown sludge bubbles, then move with caution back through the beached toys and hand her a mug with a large red S snaking up it.

Terri puts it down in silence, pulls a cigarette from the packet outlined on the front of her shirt, leaps up and bangs a frisking hand quickly over herself, one, two and behind searching for her Bic lighter. She finds it and flops down knowing the amorphous shape of the bean bag will yield to receive her.

— We are conditioned from birth! she says, wide-eyed as though she has just found this tablet new carved. — Fed myths. Maternal instinct for example. We have to get rid of these myths!

— Okay. I am bored with Terri's conversation and consider her statement tactless in the extreme. I stare out the picture window and count the telephone wires, a process I have found soothing since childhood when, trapped in the dentist's chair owing to thin enamel, I counted the wires as they shimmered and danced beyond the window distorted by the moving air above the gas flame on Mr Falner's round glass table. Sixteen there were.

— Do you want this baby? demands Terri. Twelve. Terri is leaning forward for emphasis, her elbows denting the thighs below her brief shorts.

— Yes I say.

— There you are see! Terri's finger jabs through the exhaled smoke. — You won't admit it. Why shouldn't you *say* you don't want it?

I maintain my bloated dignity.

— We've only got two I mutter.

— How will you manage without your salary? What about the mortgage?

— Oh shut up I say.

Terri regroups. — And you're so hopeless at it she says.

My face flames. I might burst. — We've got to love one another! I shout.

Terri and David are our best friends, a situation forced on us in a sense, though not entirely, by the fact that we are neighbours and David and Sam are colleagues. We know each other very well. They know as I do that Sam scratches himself when agitated. We have camped together, swum naked, so each man knows which garment each woman gropes for first when dressing. By common consent these intimacies lie buried.

Sam is an amiable man and for this I am grateful being diminished and muddled by anger at a personal level. He loves children. I mean all children. He is a better student than I am of the anthropology of children, of their nature, chants, rituals, taboos.

— This old man he played one, he played knick knack on my drum, he bellows as the Cortina spins along the motorway, its radial tyres shooting the water sideways into splayed fountains. Tom and Mick yabber in the back. Predatory as wekas they dispute Leggo pieces. Sam attempts diversion.

— Look! Look kids! he yells. — The wipers are conducting! He turns them faster. This old man hots up to hysteria. — This old man he plays one he plays . . .

— Just watch the road I moan.

— I am watching the road. I am *driving*.

The snarls in the back have gone underground.

— Let's all sing I cry.

— And he played upon a *ladel*, a *ladel*, a *ladel* I hoot in imitation of the fruity baritone. — And his name was Aken Drum.

Tom has achieved the piece. Mick bounces on buttocks stiffened by rage.

I went to Sunday School as a child. We assembled for instruction in the Church Hall. With Miss Harty. Her tongue was purple because she licked her biro, her gentleness a balm. Each attendance was enhanced by the award of a card depicting a text. *Love thy Neighbour* was particularly attractive. Wreathed with forget-me-nots two dismembered hands clasped each other in eternal amity. My mother also stressed the virtues of neighbourliness. — Don't touch the coconut bumblebees she told my eager hand. — They're for Mrs Esdale. No no not the sponge. That's for someone else.

An Englishman and his wife rented the cottage next to Uncle Fred's bach one summer. My mother placed six downy peaches on their sharp leaves and handed me the willow pattern. — Run in with these to Mr and Mrs Ormondsley. I trailed across the paspalum bearing gifts and knocked on the weathered door. It jerked open as Mrs Ormondsley tugged. A puff of rouge had slipped on one cheek. — These are for you I mumbled. — Oh she said in embarrassed surprise, pale hands reaching to receive. — How kind. Thank you. I turned to skid home. As the door closed I heard her husband's booming bittern cry. — Good God. Are the natives being friendly?

It is Saturday evening and David and Terri have arrived with two sixpacks. We sit on the deck and I hope Mick will not appear trailing his piece of blanket and wanning a dring.

David and Sam are discussing their colleague Charles who also lectures at the medical school. They don't like him.

— The bastard's got legs on his stomach from crawling. Count the times you've seen him at it! Just count *up*! says David, flinging himself back in the director's chair with force.

— Man's a total shit. Sam pulls the tab from his can and drops it back inside. He leans forward, squinting into the can with interest.

— I like him says Terri.

90

The two men swing to her in outrage.

You never know with Terri. She has an empirical selection process. The judgemental litmus paper she uses to test if people are within the pH range of her approval seems to follow no known rules. Those outside the range are irrelevant. I love her.

— He's very intelligent she says. — An interesting talker.

— Oh he can *talk* snaps David.

Terri's chin lifts.

David consolidates. — In a minute you'll be saying he interviews well!

Terry sweeps into a sulk. Her hair falls forward.

— Do y'know David continues, I don't think I've ever had a *sandwich* with the bugger that he hasn't quoted Medawar. Not once.

— Well there you are. Sam is pleased with his friend David.

— You've put your finger on it. The man hasn't an original thought in his head. Can't think . . .

Their delight in each other expands in the evening air.

David sums up. — The man's a lightweight. Second class brain.

In my sad sorrow I see the organ being reslotted lower on the intellectual tennis ladder.

This brain is not sloppy like those on butchers' slabs but firm like the one at the DSIR. Mr Burke took the whole class to an Open Day. I remember the human brain. It sat, a dirty convoluted ivory carving in a shallow dish of formalin on which floated specks of dust. The capillaries etching its surface were threads of black. I stared at it for a long time. One day I will die. One day I will not exist. It was an educational visit.

Rangitoto deepens to blue-black. David's extended foot scoops the remainder of the pack within reach of his hand. He pulls out a can and lifts it up. Our heads nod or shake in answer to his raised eyebrow. The rhythms of our shared times continue.

Later though as Sam and I edge around each other in

the bathroom I find that some of his love for David has leaked. He is muttering pejorative statements about him as he cleans his teeth and I slap Ponds on my dry skin.

— Why've you gone off him? I ask, slamming the stuff under my chin with the back of a hand.

Sam spits; slurps water from the tap into his mouth, spits again then swirls the water around the basin with the heel of his hand. He straightens to tell me.

— I didn't like what he said about Lange he says. He bangs a towel about his face.

— He's said exactly the same thing about Bassett.

Sam glares at me over the towel. — Bassett's a different thing again he says. — As you very well know.

I have assumed Bassett's iniquities. My eyes blink from behind his spectacles. My lips are pursed in his anger.

We fall into bed.

I will explain later. Sam will understand.

I haven't had a chance yet. Terri and David are with us again even though it's their turn because I haven't got round to organising a baby-sitter. As part of my commitment that we must all love one another I have made an effort with the food. Proper yeast dough in the pizza. Salad of mixed leaves. Fennel.

But the evening does not flower.

Sam, usually so amiable, is edgy. He has heard a rumour that the American scientific journal to which he has submitted his latest paper now demands 'acceptance fees' for the articles it publishes. This infuriates him, especially as he has no way of knowing if the rumour is true. Or that the paper will be accepted. He scratches frequently. He returns to the topic like a tongue to a lost filling. He drinks more than usual, he mutters imprecations, he bores.

After the real coffee he stands up. — You haven't seen the orchids lately have you Terri? he says.

— Yes says Terri. She also is restless. David, who lectures in Body Systems, has just delivered one of his periodic bursts

92

on the precise physiological and anatomical effects of
cigarette smoking. Terri's hands move in her lap.

— That new cymbidium's out says Sam. — Come and
see it.

Terri is not surprised at this invitation.

— O.K. she says, unfolding herself from the bean chair.
She drifts after him as he moves across the kitchen to the
back porch. The back door clunks.

David smiles at me. He is a nice man David. I have always
said so.

— Shall I put something on the stereo he says. I nod.

— How about the old Kreutzer? — Mmmmm I say. We
sit in companionable silence as the music surges around
us and I wish I liked the noise more. I lean back and we
smile at each other.

Terri and Sam are away a long time but I don't mind
because of my commitment. Nor does David. He moves
to sit beside me on the sofa. His simian face is kind. His
charm laps me.

— Pregnant women turn me on he says. I understand this.
I wish to stroke the long silky black hairs on his wandering
arm. I need to make sure that they all lie the same way.
It is essential. I have felt this necessity before but never
as keenly.

Sam and Terri appear around the free-standing brick
fireplace, having come in through the front door. Sam is
talking over his shoulder to Terri. Their appearance is that
of two actors whose entrance indicates a wealth of shared
experience offstage.

David's hand has moved down again to my stomach. I
grimace wildly. — Get off I mouth. I bounce agitatedly in
a futile attempt to dislodge the hand. It has a life of its
own this hand, as autonomous as those of *Love thy Neighbour*.

Sam swings round.

— Take your hand off my wife! he shouts.

The anachronism leaves us all speechless with shame for
Sam. I heave myself into a more upright position and redrape

the erogenous zone. My eyes are down for Sam not for me. I am very intent on my pleating fingers. The hand has gone. The Beethoven has finished.

The best defence is attack. — God you're a prick! David shouts, leaping up. — You get Ann like this. He glares down at my stomach, now suddenly erogenous free. — You ask me here, bore me shitless, disappear for hours with my wife then come back and abuse *me*! His voice rises at the temerity of the man.

Terri has moved to the uncurtained window during this outburst. Three pairs of eyes turn to her. She is the needle of our emotional barometer. What will she do to set us fair again? Nothing. She stares out into the dark as though she is reading it. Her back is beautiful. The atmosphere sparking. I love her.

— I'll get some coffee I say, banal as a TV ad. I start heaving myself up from the sofa. Pushing up with my hands I give a little levering kick with my feet as I reach the edge.

— No! David's firm hand on my shoulder topples me back. — We're going. Come on Terri. The flared hems of her satin trousers swing as she turns. She is silent. It is extremely effective.

They sweep across the Berber to the front door, escorted by a flourish of attendant lords and ladies. A tumbling dwarf.

The door is not slammed.

— Wow I say.

Sam turns on me.

We get to bed somehow. Sam is so enraged he is almost sobbing. — The man's a shit! he says again. The sibilant hate spits out. — Sam I say. He jumps into bed and rolls over immediately. Silver from the street light edges the curtain. It doesn't matter. It doesn't matter. Wisdom unfurls inside my head like one of those Japanese paper flowers in a glass of clear water. They came in shells, Japanese pipis. If I had one I could demonstrate and Sam would understand. Instead we lie side by side after our hard bruising game ticking like time bombs. Our feet touch the base board. The silence skids around the dark room. I open my mouth several times. I am about to explain it all. — Sam I say. His breathing thickens into explosive nasal snorts. He lies on his back, his mouth wide open in a silent shriek. He sleeps, one connubial arm flung across whatever it is that lives inside me.

Tuataras

They fascinated him, the hatching tuataras. Inch-long dragons pecking their way to a wider world. Shells are expected to enclose endearing and vulnerable balls of yellow, grey, or black fluff, but these were different. Leathery, wrinkled like dirty white gloves, the discarded ones resembled something unattractive and crumpled in the bottom of a laundry basket. Each shell had a number written on it with a felt pen. Charles Renshawe opened the inner glass door of the incubator and picked up 18 with care. The occupant had made little progress since his last inspection. The minuscule eyes stared, their sudden blink startling as a wink from a blank face. They peered at him above a jagged rim, the body still completely enclosed.

Charles despised anthropomorphism in any form. Dogs with parasols teetering on their hind legs, advertisements in which chimpanzees jabbered their delight at cups of tea, made him very angry. — What happened to the Mesozoic reptiles? he asked the head.

He replaced the egg quickly, closed the double doors of the incubator, then turned to watch the juveniles which had hatched during the last week.

They were housed in a display case the base of which was covered with a deep layer of dry compost. The tuatara-hatching project was the work of one of his brighter honours students and had been almost too successful. — We'll have them coming out our ears soon, Doctor, said Mrs Blume, crooning and pecking at the department's computer in the back room.

Charles relit his pipe yet again and counted them. Still eleven. The juveniles were exact miniatures of the adult forms except that they had no upstanding spines along the midline of their backs. Three of them had red dots between their eyes, the identification system of another student's research. This too pleased Charles. Class distinction among the archaic reptiles.

You hardly ever saw them moving. Their immobility was one of the things which fascinated him. He stared at one which was standing on three legs, willing it to ground the fragment of claw. He thought of the toads he had seen on an overnight stop in Guam on his way to present a paper at a Royal Society conference in Tokyo. They had appeared from this tropical dark, dozens of them, to squat motionless on the floodlit concrete path beneath his host's window. Suddenly one would move. Hop. Hop hop hop. Hop. Hop hop. Then resume its rock-like squat, immobile as a programmed chess piece between moves.

Charles glanced at his watch. He had had his five minutes. He gave a faint sigh, turned off the light and returned through Mrs Blume's office to his own shambles. He sat at the desk which was submerged beneath piles of examination papers and resumed his marking. He worked steadily for an hour, ballpoint in hand, ticking, marking, deciding.

His laugh crashed through the silence of the still building, an explosion of pleasure as he rocked back in his chair. He had used the metaphor 'a dishcover of membrane bones' in an unfortunate attempt at clarification in a second-year lecture. He remembered standing in front of a hundred faces, the Asians and their tape recorders intent in the front rows, the rest a haze, a sea of uninterest. Every one of the papers already marked had chanted back the inane phrase. This candidate wrote with authority about a dishcloth of membrane bones. Charles read on, his heart sinking. You would think they would pick up something. At least have a glimmer. Hopeless. Hopeless.

At two a.m. he gave up. He stretched his arms above his head in capitulation, yawned wide as the goodnight kiwi, marched out of the mess and locked the door.

He lay very still when he woke next morning, then shut his eyes again quickly. Marking, he thought. That's all. Marking. Then he remembered. Last night had been bad. Very bad. So bad that he had picked up the pile of papers and retreated to his office at the University leaving Rhona red-faced and outraged at the table, abandoned among the chop bones and wilting salad. Charles heaved himself up in the bed. His thin hair stood up from his head in a caricature of fright, his myopic eyes searched with his groping fingers for the spectacles on the bedside table. No sound. Rhona must have finished in the bathroom. Her knuckles tapped against his door. — Out, said his sister, stumping back along the passage to her room.

She was still a good-looking woman. Her fine papery skin lay virtually unlined across the 'good bones' of her face. Her grey hair was puffed and gentle about her face except when Ashley did it too tight. — Don't worry, Charles said, It'll grow out. — All very well for you, replied Rhona, her eyes snapping. And of course it was all very well for him, it had no effect whatsoever, even if she had had it dyed purple as she'd once threatened to do.

Rhona had been the toast of the town when towns still had toasts. She had appeared frequently among the photographs on the Social Page of slim girls 'escorted' by haunted-looking young men with jug ears. Her face, even in the smudged print, was flawless, her eyes large, the corners of her mouth curving upwards with pleasure. And she was friendly too, and generous. Often she would hiss at one of the young men hovering around her, Go on, go and dance with Leonie. She's been there all night. And the youth would retreat and return to be rewarded by a smile, that smile.

As the years passed the lesser toasts married, their nuptial photographs splashing through the pages of *The Free Lance*. 'Broad acres united', sang the caption beneath the bucolic groom and the hysterical-looking girl clinging to his arm. 'Titian bride' followed 'Twins unite in double ceremony', and still Rhona was unmarried. Nobody could understand it.

Charles was not interested. He was grateful to his sister for being a success and thus freeing him from responsibilities often hissed upon other young men. — And look after your sister. Especially the Supper Waltz. He flatly refused to go to dances. Mrs Renshawe, a strong-minded woman, threatened, cajoled, pleaded. Charles wore her down. 'I am not going to the Combined Dance.' 'I am not going to the Leavers' Dance.' 'I am not going.' Endless scraps of paper bearing such messages haunted Mrs Renshawe in the ball season. They greeted her from every box, container, drawer. They confronted her as she reached for an ivory tip, fluttered from the inside of her rolled napkin, lay beneath the knives in the knife drawer, even, she found once with a slight shock, fell from inside the toilet roll. Defeated, Mrs Renshawe decided that Charles would be better copy as an embryo intellectual. And he was a boy.

Charles fulfilled his mother's predictions. A good student, his interest in Zoology was quickened in the sixth form by one of the few effective teachers left behind during the war. Mr Beson was 4F, unfit for active service. He taught science, taught it well, and Charles was hooked. He enrolled at Otago as soon as he left school and majored in Chemistry and Zoology before going Overseas for post-graduate study.

It never occurred to Charles not to go home from Dunedin

each holiday. He was quite happy in Hobson Street. He was quite happy anywhere. And besides, he knew he was not staying. He drove his mother about the town, opened the door of the Buick for her as he had been instructed since childhood, stowed her parcels with care, smiled at her when she had finished her shopping and asked with a professional backwards chuck of his head, Home, Mum? He accompanied his father to the Club occasionally, but not often. He stood around politely as his father played snooker in the Billiard Room with Neville Frensham, and the light glinted on the bottles in the bar and the tension heightened and Charles thought what a balls-aching waste of time it all was.

Neville Frensham was a stockbroker in the same firm as his father. Younger, but not a great deal. He and Mr Renshawe walked home together after work and his father often asked Frensham in for a drink. Charles remembered the man, relaxed, at his ease in a large chair, the evening sunlight falling on the hand which held a full glass, a 'mixed trough' of dahlias and Michaelmas daisies on the mantlepiece above him. Mrs Renshawe sat smiling at him from a smaller chair. She liked large, decisive men with firm handshakes. Charles and his father sat on the padded window seat with cushions at their backs. Rhona, calm, still, beautiful, was perched on the edge of a spindly unpadded thing. She proffered nuts while Charles poured the drinks, the women's gin and tonics in small cut glasses, the men's whiskies in things twice the size; strong, hefty containers you could get a grip on. He saw Mr Frensham shake his head in rejection at the nuts. He patted his stomach, smiling up at Rhona.

— And do you know what he said? he asked. Welcomed after toil, Mr Frensham was enjoying himself. Four pairs of eyes watched him, four faces were attentive. The saga concerned a friend of his son's, a lad about seventeen, to whom Mr Frensham had offered a whisky. He had then enquired about diluents. — And do you know what he said?

100

He asked for ginger ale! exploded Mr Frensham. He rocked
back in his flowery chair, a wary eye on his glass. — I ask
you! Shock was registered. Excessive from Mr Renshawe,
milder from his wife. None from Charles, who was refusing
to play. His usual chameleon-like attribute of melding into
any social decor seemed to have deserted him. He stared
moodily into his beer. Rhona's smile blessed them all.
   — Well you can imagine! Mr Frensham gave a little kick
with both feet in his excitement. — I'll give you a whisky
if you want one, I said, but I'm damned if I'm going to
let any callow youth ruin my hard-found whisky with lolly
water. I told him! He got short shift from me.
   — Shrift, said Charles.
The bristling bad tempered eyebrows leapt at him.
   — Pardon?
   — The word's shrift, said Charles.

He always enjoyed seeing Rhona, who was now more
beautiful than ever. Her pale skin seemed to be illuminated
from within. He supposed her capillaries must lie close to
the surface, but had the wit not to say so. They had the
ease together of those who expect and require nothing from
each other. She was still rather notably unmarried.
   The next day they trailed upstairs after Sunday Lunch,
Rhona in front, Charles two steps behind. She stopped and
gripped the newel post on the landing.
   — Charles, she said.
   — Yes, he said, his eyes on her hand.
   — Come along to my room for a minute.
   — O.K.
It was a pleasant room, low-ceilinged, a small window
framed with flowered curtains. He watched the leaves
blowing about on the striped lawn below them. His father
appeared with the hand mower and began shaving the
stripes. Charles pulled the curtain slightly to screen himself,
and smiled at Rhona. She took no notice.
   — Sit down, she said, patting the bed beside her. The

101

bedcover was the same flowered pattern of poppies, daisies, and cornflowers. A pastoralist's nightmare he thought, and opened his mouth to say so.

— Charles, said Rhona.

— Yes? he sat down beside her and crossed his legs. The bed tipped them towards each other. Charles moved slightly.

— Charles, I want to tell you something.

— Yes, said Charles.

She seemed remarkably agitated. She scrambled up onto the pillow and hugged her knees, wrapping the Liberty's skirt tight around them.

— Aren't you going to ask me what it is? she demanded.

— You'll tell me, he said.

— Oh! The gasp was a rasping intake of air.

— I'm having an affair with Neville Frensham, she said.

— Oh, said Charles.

— Is that all you've got to say! Her blues eyes seared him. His skin prickled.

—He's married isn't he? said Charles miserably.

— Of course he's married, you clot. That's why it's an affair.

An affair, thought Charles. Good heavens. And with that sod. He thought of that hand, that stomach.

— Why are you telling me? he asked.

— God knows, said Rhona, and burst into tears all over him.

She went Overseas soon afterwards. Charles was home when they farewelled her on the *Rangitoto*. They inspected the cabin she was to share with her friend Penelope, large, fair, a good sort. Rhona's side of the cabin was deep in flowers, hot spikes of gladioli were piled upon her bunk, the tiny inadequate shelves spilled over with pyramid-shaped 'arrangements' in posy bowls. Charles watched his sister's face as she read the card attached to a large bouquet of fleshy white orchids.

— Whoever sent those, dear? said Mrs Renshawe.

— The girls from the office, replied Rhona. Charles removed his spectacles, blew on them and wiped them with care. When they left the ship Rhona clung to him, sobbing, hiccoughing with the abandoned despair of a lost child. Mrs Renshawe was puzzled.

Rhona did various jobs in London. She was sacked from Harrods for suggesting to a customer who complained of the high price of the handkerchiefs that perhaps she should shop elsewhere. She trained at an exclusive interior design shop and developed the languid hauteur required. She was hardworking, used her initiative, and they enjoyed her slightly flattened vowels. She lived with English girls which pleased her mother. — What is the point, Mrs Renshawe asked her friend Rita, of going twelve thousand miles across the world to flat with Penelope Parsons?

Rhona wrote cheerful letters home which told nothing. Charles read them and was glad she was happy. They exchanged postcards. He collected all the interesting ones, the bottle at Paeroa, the floral clock at Napier, diners with their mouths open stuffing food at the Hermitage. Rhona replied with reproductions of naked sculptures from the Louvre, the Uffizi, wherever. 'Having wonderful time. Wish you were here.' Charles liked her.

She came home occasionally. She was now elegant as well as beautiful. She was invited to meals with all her married friends and played on floors with her many godchildren to whom she gave expensive English-type presents. Corals, for example, for the little girls to wear with their party frocks. Large Dinky Toy milk floats and rubbish collection vans which the little boys did not recognize, and which had to be explained and demonstrated by Rhona from England.

She came home when their father died, and two years later when they moved Mrs Renshawe into a home. — I'm not coming home to look after her, she said, glaring at

Charles. — Good God, no, he answered. — And you can't can you? — No, said Charles. He had done his best but fortunately it was not enough.

Charles stayed on, rattling around in the Hobson Street house where he had lived since he returned to take up his appointment in Wellington. He gardened, he visited his mother, he invited people for meals. — Anyone who can read can cook, he said, though the hard part was having it all ready at the same countdown. He enjoyed his work and was good at it. He was glad his mother had given up on grandchildren.

He and Rhona never discussed Neville Fransham. He wondered whether to tell her when he died, but did nothing. Someone else would and anyway it was forty years ago. Good God.

He was astounded when Rhona's letter arrived. 'I am returning to New Zealand. Presumably it's all right by you if I come to Hobson Street. Mother can't last much longer and I should be there. Anyway, I want to come home. Very odd. Obviously I'll take over the cooking etc. It might be rather fun. Two of us bumbling towards extinction together. Much love, Rhona.'

Charles thought hard, his mind scurrying for solutions. He thought of cabling 'Don't come. Have made alternative arrangements.' Or just plain 'No. Don't.' But how could he? Under the terms of their father's will she had an equal share in the house. And anyway, how could he?

She came. She stayed. She moved into their mother's bedroom, a large room with a fireplace in one corner, a dressing table on which Mrs Renshawe's silver brushes still sat, a high bed covered with a crocheted bedspread and a long box thing covered in flowered cretonne. When he carried Rhona's suitcases up she had touched the box with the tip of her small pointed shoe. — Good God, she said — the ottoman. What on earth would *Zaharis Interior Design* say? She flung her squashy leather bag on the bed and flopped down beside it. She stared up at Charles with something like panic. He was puffing slightly. — Mr Parkin begged me, she said. — They didn't want me to leave you know. Then why the hell did you, thought Charles, disliking himself. He put an arm around the slightly padded shoulder of her Italian knit and pressed slightly. She buried her fluffy grey head against his jacket for a moment and sniffed.

— Oh well, she said standing up, silver bangles jangling. — Is there any sherry?

But things got worse. He could have told her. He should have told her.

Charles stumped down the stairs, his right hand touching the wall lightly at intervals in a gesture imitated by his students. He turned left through the hall and padded into the kitchen. Rhona was sitting at the table with her back to the sun in the chair in which he had always sat, reading the paper.

— Good morning, said Charles.
— Hullo. She didn't look up.
He lifted the small blue and white striped teapot from the bench. — Old or new? he said. She glanced up briefly.
— Old, she said. Charles opened the window and emptied the teapot onto the rose beneath. He pressed down the red flag of the Russell Hobbs kettle. A plastic bag, its contents weeping and bloody, lay beside it. Charles poked it.
— What's this?
She glanced up, frowning. — What?
He poked again. — This.
— Plums, said Rhona.
— Ah.
Charles made tea, poured himself a cup and pulled out a chair which raked loudly on the faded green vinyl. A blackbird sang, defining its territory. He glanced out across the sunlit lawn. There it was as usual, singing its proprietorial

heart out from the spindly kauri in the next door garden. Charles sat down and helped himself to cornflakes, refolding Rhona's open packet of muesli and placing it on the bench. — Which is the whole milk? he asked. Head down, still reading, Rhona handed him a jug embellished with the crowned image of George VI. She had finished her breakfast and was smoking the first of her day's cigarettes. She was a tidy smoker, meticulous in the removal of butts, the emptying of ashtrays. Unlike Charles whose pipe dottle and matchstick-filled messes overflowed throughout the house. He poured milk onto the cereal and attacked the mush with quick scooping movements of his spoon, herding it into his mouth. He bonged a striped cotton napkin at his face and reached for the toast.

— Any chance of a piece of the paper? he asked.

Rhona swung into action, slapping and tugging at the paper as though it was putting up enormous resistance. Still clutching the overseas news page she handed a crumpled heap to Charles.

— Thank you, said Charles, smoothing and refolding the thing. They read in bristling silence for a while.

— I heard on the radio that Lange's not going to Paris, he said, raising a tentative flag of truce.

It was shot to ribbons. — Would you, snapped Rhona. — In the circumstances?

— Perhaps not, said Charles.

Rhona snorted, flicking her ash into the small brass ashtray with a quick decisive tap. She finished the cigarette and ground the glowing butt into extinction, then heaved herself up against the unstable plastic table. It rocked, slopping milky tea into Charles' saucer. She emptied the ashtray into the Pelican bag beneath the sink and reclosed the door. She remained planted in front of the sink, a strong white arm clasping the stained blue formica either side of her. Charles, from the corner of his eye, saw her put her head in her hands. Oh God he thought dully. A miasma of dread enclosed him, paralysing action, thought, threatening his very existence as a civilised thinking being.

He made an enormous effort. — What's the matter, Rhona? he said.

Rhona swung around, her pearls clasped about her plump neck, her hands clasped in agony. — It's so bloody *awful* here, she said.

Charles glared at her. Who was she to stand in his familiar old-fashioned kitchen, to breathe its slightly gas-scented air and mouth such antediluvian, anti-colonial crap?

— Are you pining for dear dirty old London? he asked.

Rhona's eyes blinked with surprise. Charles was surprised himself.

— Yes, snapped Rhona. — Yes, I am.

Charles felt rage thickening in his throat. Stronger even than his interest in the Comparative Anatomy of Vertebrates was his feeling for the land forms, the fauna and flora of the country where he grew up. When he had been a postgraduate student in England many of his New Zealand contemporaries had worked and schemed for the glittering prizes of Overseas Appointments. Charles, more able than most, had regarded these men (there were no women) as unusual genetic aberrations who could not be blamed for their imperfections. He knew he was going home and did so.

— And you're so *boring*! continued Rhona, angrily banging her wrists in search of her handkerchief.

Charles breathed out, a liberating puff of relief. — I've always been boring, he said.

Rhona slammed back to the table and crashed her behind onto the unstable silly little chair opposite him.

— Don't you care? she demanded.

— Not in the slightest, said Charles.

She thumped the table with her closed fist.

— And I suppose you're proud of that! Proud of your Intellectual Honesty! she cried. Her face, usually a pleasant sight, was mottled, despairing, damp.

— I don't bore me, said Charles mildly.

To his horror, just when Charles thought he had cushioned the trauma, siphoned off the excess, set things on an even keel again, Rhona for only the third time in his experience, burst into tears.

— You're only half a . . . She gasped. — Only half *there!*

She disintegrated before him. She laid her rounded arms on the plastic table and howled like a — like a what? Charles had never seen anything like it in his life. He stared at her. What should he do? Slap her? God forbid. Ice? Wet towels? He slipped sideways from his skittery little chair and tiptoed from the kitchen.

He felt bad about it. Very bad. Twice in twenty four hours he had abandoned a suffering human being. Charles was not an uncaring man. He gave to things. Not only to any conservation scheme however bizarre or impractical, but also to humanity. His donations to the City Mission had been regular and substantial. They had asked him to join the Board but he had declined owing to pressure of work. They quite understood.

He felt miserable all day. He chaired a Scholarship Board meeting with firm detachment. He continued with his marking, refusing as always to count how many papers remained unmarked. He lunched in the Staff Cafeteria, sitting with his salami and tomato roll, staring across the tossing windblown harbour a thousand miles away. He exchanged pleasantries with Mrs Blume who was suffering from a completely unjustified excess of work, but there you were.

He had not visited the tuataras all day. He finished his last second year paper and leaned back, reaching out a spatulate-fingered hand for the striped tobacco pouch on his desk. He tamped the tobacco into his Lovat Saddle pipe with a nicotine-stained forefinger, wiped the finger on the carpet, and lit up, puffing his pipe with the catharsis of release. After a few minutes he pushed his chair back and ambled out of his office, through Mrs Blume's room into the small laboratory which housed the tuataras.

His fingers quivered as he opened the inner glass door of the incubator. He had timed it well. Before him the tuatara which last night had been a shell, a half head with eyes, climbed out from the remnants of its shell. With a backwards flick of its fragmentary left rear leg it tossed the shell aside. The movement reminded Charles of a stripper in a Soho dive thirty years ago as she kicked aside the irrelevant sloughed-off garments beneath her feet. Charles clutched the sides of the incubator. He felt weak with pleasure. Infinitely tender he picked the newly hatched tuatara up from the incubator and enrolled it among its associates in the compost. It did nothing. It just squatted there, planted on its four angled legs, occasionally moving its head very slowly to one side or the other. Charles picked up a piece of waste paper from the bench on which the incubator stood, pulled out his ballpoint and wrote, 'Have removed No. 18 (contents of) from incubator. In display case. C.R.' He slipped the note into the incubator door as he closed it.

He stood back. A transfusion of happiness flowed through him. He had thought of something. He hurried back to his office, giving Mrs Blume no more than a perfunctory nod. He would do something. Show his concern, his love almost. He reached for the telephone and dialled his home number.
— Rhona, he said into the quacking receiver. — Would you like to see the juvenile tuataras? The babies?

Feeding the Sparrows

— Start where you like then start where you like she says
and tell me about your life.

What was it like then when I first fed them, scurrying
and leaping down the twisted paths of the Gardens leaving
caches of crumbs by the rugosa roses, the Holland
monument, Dick Seddon himself for God's sake.

Green days forty years ago I say when I was young and
something carving out a career as the lad, the sweeper-
upper the packer-into the putter-out of wholesale groceries
and believe me they are legion. I could show you caverns
of food, cool rooms of cheese with salami alongside, Nescafé
drums shaped for caterers. And a Gourmet Range, though
thought little of by the bread and butter trade who were
our bread and butter say what you like. The only lad they
ever had to pick up a broom unasked Farrer said and where
did it get me. What's the virtue in picking up unasked other
than to show that you don't have to be asked. Better to
leave the broom lying and not take the whole sodding world
on my back because that's what I did, I see now, and the
birds too as you know.

Sixteen and hefty with it. Strong lad wanted and got.
Not my first job either. That was sorting for blows in a

factory. There was a sign where we whinged and queued for pay. — Work hard eight hours a day and don't worry and in time you may become the boss and have all the worry. And all the money and a house in the hills and a car with a musical horn the sod. I lost my first pay envelope you remember a thing like that. And bought a green pork pie hat with the second. After that they blur.

I felt, I see it now, that no one else could do anything properly. Not just as well as me. Almost at all. Whatever it was — the broom I snatched from the floor, the shelves I monkeyed up desperate to stock the top stuff though all of it within reach of the smallest dairy owner and some are small my word, the sari ladies. That was why, I think now. That was why, though it's hard to say. The books I read no one read, the poems that stay in snatches upset the others if I said them. There's not much poetry in a suburban branch so it's down to the Central and you have to be quick in the weekend for a chair in the sun from the winos.

I heard them at work talking through the years. I heard them saying sodding storeman for God's sake. — Not number one junior to Jesus. — Look Denny I can stack any fool can stack. I can lug cartons Denny, I got m'letters. — Piss off, y'wanker, get off my back, all that they say and more but still I feel and still I know and still it is inside eating me that they can't, not properly. Not unless I see it, not unless I watch them. Better if I've done it myself then I know.

I know what they mean though. I see myself. I stand at the check-out and the wooden trolleys line up packed teetering high for the dairies, low for the private customers, and my eyes are everywhere. I take the goods off for the girl at the computer to sweep with her ray gun and I see my face in the mirror behind the check out and it looks like the worried face of someone maybe a relation. There is black hair in the neck of a white shirt sprigged with brown and a heavy duty red apron over it and the face of this

111

man is anxious and his hair shoots off his head and it is leaping straight upwards black and anxious and he chews his lip this guy. — Calm down says Diane or May or whoever. — Calm down Denny. But they whisper, Really kinky eh.

The same in the Canteen if you can call it a Canteen, a room at the back. I get an instant from the machine and I have a cheese scone always the same from The Lilac next door and I read Prufrock from the back pocket of my shorts, summer and winter under the red apron though I take that off in the canteen. — I grow old . . . I grow old . . . I shall wear the bottoms of my trousers rolled, and I see the old guy in England at the seaside never the beach like here. Always I do the same each day. I sit down and I place my Rothmans on my right side hand and my Bic lighter opposite and my scone plate in front of my book behind that flat for reading and the cup at my right hand. I lift each thing up and put it down several times and no one else comes to my table which is how I like it, and Jeeze they say but let them it is how I like it.

— The birds she says.

— Yes?

— You fed them?

— Yes.

— For how many years.

I have been asked so many times I know straight off.

— Forty, I say.

— And when did you . . . ? Her eyes are green. Her hand is still.

— Start on my back?

— Yes.

— Thirty years ago.

— And the couple from the Embassy?

I say nothing.

— When did they?

So I say it again, all I've said again and again and again. It was my own way. I made it up. It was mine. I knew if anyone saw they would try and they wouldn't do it right

so when I thought of it I took my bag of crumbs in behind
the shed. I get off the bus at the shelter, Glenmore Street,
the covered one with fretwork, cross the street on the
crossing that's what it's for, why not use the thing, and
down the dog leg past the azaleas. Make sure no one is
in sight and slip behind the mower shed, you know where
they keep the mowers. I knew if anyone saw they'd try
and I knew they'd get it wrong. I bend down see like this,
back quite flat and very carefully I put the crumbs on my
back and the sparrows are strung out waiting on the
guttering each morning, well almost, for thirty years. I am
very quiet, there is no sound but the birds or sometimes
a creak from the tin roof. When I am still they come down
and peck the crumbs from my back and I feel the gentle
bill pricks through my parka though you know there's never
a hole. The slightest noise even on the path say and they
hoosh up and the pecks stop till quiet again and they return.
Ten minutes I give them no more then I stand up and they
shoot off in all directions they know it's over, but they come
back when I'm still to peck the crumbs from the ground.

This day I am feeding them, the smell of moss damp
in the air. April it was and I know there is someone else
there even though I don't hear because the birds fly up.
Still down I turn my head and I see four trouser legs, two
dark grey and two light grey and I know it is them, the
man and his wife from the Embassy.

— Then?

I have seen them often on my way home. I walk across
the bridge though it wasn't there when I started at the
warehouse. I have seen them walking hand in hand in the
gardens for years in their Mao suits smiling. It was his suit
which was lighter grey. Her hair was clamped to her head
with dark clips, her walk was a shuffle. People liked them
holding hands and smiling, everyone smiled back, the
joggers, the strollers, the kids even in prams.

So when I saw the legs I knew but it didn't make it any
better. I stood up and stared at them not smiling. They

smiled and bowed and crept away still hand in hand down by the side of the shed but I felt sick you know sick and I was right.

They must have been practising. A fortnight later I came up the main path through the cemetery on my way home. I wanted a leak so I hopped behind the old fashioned roses. (And what were they doing anyway that morning behind the mower shed?) He was bent over, the little guy his back flat his hands on his knees and she was sprinkling crumbs on his back and they were two chattering and sniggering kids with secrets.

— And?

The sparrows shot off as I yanked him upwards with one hand hefting the back of his Mao collar and flung him forward on the concrete. He crashed face downwards, arms and legs sprawled like a free fall and she screamed and rushed to him, keening and crooning I suppose his name. She lifted his head and saw his face and ran away screaming and I stayed there with him till it was quiet and the birds came back.

I Want to Get Out, I Said

Her mother sat very straight beside the empty driver's seat. Mary leaned forward and inspected three tiny sacs of loose skin on the back of the neck in front of her.

— You should have them off, Mum.

— What?

— The things on the back of your neck.

— They're not doing any harm.

— They're not doing any good.

— Be quiet, Mary. Her grandfather sat motionless, an assemblage of crumpled clothes, a smell of cigarettes and airless nights.

Mary ground her behind deeper into the back seat and stared out the window at the dust. Who did he think he was? Some deposed Emperor for God's sake, instead of which . . . She moved nearer the window to avoid contact with his hairy jacket but his shape flowed after her, overlaying her side of the car.

— I'm getting out.

— It's very dusty.

— I know it's dusty. I want to get out.

Her mother's sigh drifted through from the front seat.

— It's not my fault.

115

BARBARA ANDERSON

— I didn't say it was.
— Nobody could expect two punctures.
— I would have thought you could. On a road like this.
— You wanted to see the forest.
— Not much.
— You said.
— All right, all right I said.
Her grandfather heaved his right buttock from the back seat and extracted a flattened cigarette packet from his trouser pocket. His trembling fingers lit a cigarette then held the match to Mary's face for her to blow out. She could kill him, quite seriously she could kill him.
— I want to get out, I said.
Her mother made an odd little sound, somewhere between a grunt and another sigh. She opened the car door and heaved herself out, shaking her cotton skirt from behind sticky knees. She held the front seat forward for Mary, then stamped her jandals on the road, causing plumes of dust to rise around her purple ankles.
— It's very dusty. She stared up through the towering trees.
— We've seen them anyway, she said.

It hadn't started too badly.
— There's no reason why we can't do things as a family just because, her mother had said. — I'll do the driving, well mostly, and you and Sam can take a turn. If you want to, on the . . . The sentence remained unfinished, the unspoken 'easy bits' left hanging. It was the first summer since their father had left. He had come home from the paint shop one lunch hour as Mary and her mother sat at the kitchen table sorting plums.
— Dad. Her mother's head lifted as though she had caught his scent, not the sound of his boots on the concrete. He kicked open the fly door, nodded at them as he dropped the red plastic lunch box on the table and strode the few steps to the bathroom. Silence flowed after him, widening.

116

Mary's mother bent her head and studied each plum more carefully. Jam? Bottling? Eating?

He came back after some time, the sculpted waves of his grey hair still damp from the comb. With one leg he pulled a chair out from the table and dropped onto it without a backward glance. He picked up one of the ripe plums and turned it over and over, staring at it as though it might tell him something.

— Sandra and I are going to Oz, he said.
— Sandra who?
— For Christ's sake! Is that all . . .?
— No no Jim I meant . . . I didn't mean . . .

For months afterward her mother behaved like a sheep which had blundered into the wrong race and become separated from the rest of the mob. Any attempt to understand the calamity which had befallen her was useless. She seemed befuddled, a bewildered old ewe banging a woolly head against the rails. All she wanted was to be back with the other girls. Together again. Discussing how Des wouldn't look at beetroot, and as for Jim, they all knew about Jim's eating habits. And his other habits. Mary knew, while still at school. Her mother, that true cliché of the deserted wife, was the last to know. She never blamed Jim, she didn't blame her friend Sandra, she just knew that somehow it had all gone wrong. She had missed some sign, some friendly signal which should have alerted her. Her eyes filled often with hot easy tears. — We were so happy though, she said. Mary wanted to shake her. To shout and scream that it wasn't her mother's silly fault if her husband dumped her for Sandra fat Hatton.

Her grandfather had always been there. His presence seeped through the quiet house as he sat calm and benign in the one comfortable chair in the sitting room. He moved slightly, unbuttoned his cardigan or lifted a foot and replaced it as Jim crashed up the back steps each evening, slamming the

117

fly door which sent its shuddering clatter through the rooms.
— G'day Pops.
— Good evening.
Still.
— Go a beer?
— Thank you.
No one knew his reaction to Jim's departure. He tried
to comfort his daughter, patting her shoulder with tentative
little movements of a long-fingered pale hand.
— There. There.

Mary's brother Sam also kept his own counsel. He was
sixteen when his father left, a tall gentle boy who spent
a lot of his time lying prone beneath the 1957 De Soto
he was stripping on the concrete beside the circular
clothesline. As Mary stepped between his outstretched legs
one evening, she heard him grunt. She put down her heavy
office bag.
— Yeah?
— Hang on. He rolled out from under the chassis of the
dismembered car and reached for an oily rag. He began
wiping each finger.
— Well.
He looked at her, squinting into the sun, a streak of oil
above his upper lip.
— Do you want to go up north? he said.
They listened to the thudding chatter of the Fitzgerald's
old mower gathering itself together, then the change in
tone as it was propelled into action. — No, said Mary.
— Well?
— We have to.
— Aw shit. He wiped a final finger. — You know what
he'll be like.
— Yes.
— Well then I said.
— She wants to.
— Why?

— Ask her.

His eyes were slits.

— Stuck in the car with him.

— Yes.

— All that bloody way.

— Yes.

He said nothing more, but dropped his head till he lay full length on the concrete, then rolled quickly beneath the car. A hand came out groping for the transistor. Mary bent to move it to him. She touched the sole of one grimy foot with the toe of her strappy sandal, opened the fly door and stepped quickly inside. It snatched like a greedy hand.

It hadn't been too bad. Not so far. There was little chat in the car, and no radio. Power lines looped and slid by, measuring the Escort's mile after mile after mile progression to the north. Ice creams sank in cones, licked into nothing. Comfort stations were inspected. Occasionally her mother came out quickly, puckered lips pressed rigid in rejection.
— Drive on Sam, she said. Her father sat glaring ahead with myopic eyes.

— I've never seen the kauris, he said. — Funny that. I once lived . . . The pause lengthened. — Yes, he said.

The mosquitos struck at Paihia. Sam held out a thin arm.
— They don't bit me.

His grandfather continued anointing himself with care.
— They do, he said, — but you're not allergic to them.

— I'd know if I'd been bitten.

— What's that then?

— What?

— There.

— That!

— It would be lovely if we had a boat, said his Mother.

The sun poured over Mary's shoulders the next morning as she watched her mother pay the motel bill, smiling and bobbing at the emaciated woman behind the desk. Through

119

the open door she saw her grandfather light a cigarette. The woman lifted a brass urn of blush-pink artificial orchids, rubbed the formica beneath it with the closed fist which terminated the twisted ropes of her arm, and put it down again. Her tan had leached to fawn.

— It gets in the drapes, she said. — I'd rather have ten non smokers any day. It's the drapes. Mary's grandfather peered at her. — Drapes?

— Thank you. Thank you. His daughter took his arm and guided him to the back seat of the car. — Off you go Sam.

The Escort spurted forward. It leapt at the cattle stop, knocking the hibiscus which offered its red plate-like blossoms to the sun.

— Sam, said his mother.

Miles later the car swung left.

— Is this right?

— Yes.

— Oh.

The gravel road deteriorated, small stones sprayed from beneath the wheels, dust rose in swirls around the shimmering heat of the car.

— I'll drive, Sam, said his mother.

Sam's hands tightened on the wheel.

— Sam.

— Put your window up, Sam, said his grandfather. The sneeze was a volcanic, roaring explosion. — Handkerchief! He flapped an angry hand at the box of tissues Mary handed him. — Useless! Useless! he gasped, then grabbed a handful and made quick bonging movements all over his streaming face. Discarded tissues drifted to the floor. — Dust, he said. — Dust. The car slewed in the gravel and lurched forward, hobbling.

— Puncture, said Sam.

They piled out of the car in silence. Mary helped Sam unload the boot. The pile of holiday gear grew, incongruous and hateful among the grey daisies on the verge. A bird sang in triumph above them as Sam dragged out the spare tyre and bounced it on the road. — Pretty shot, he said, as he attacked the hubcap of the failed wheel.

They were more talkative for a short while after the first puncture, the survivors exchanging brief smiles. Sam's mother brushed his neck with the back of her hand. He sat well back in the seat, his arms stiff as he swung the car into the curves. The temperature rose. The car lurched to the right again as the spare tyre collapsed.

Sam set off for Dargaville bowling the first punctured tyre in front of him, a parody of a Victorian children's book illustration. A 'car seethed past, obscured in its own dust storm. Mary's grandfather closed his eyes. The dead match fell from his fingers onto the shredded tissues.

— I want to get out, I said.

Mary's mother clambered out and held the front seat forward. Her grandfather's eyes opened.

— We're all in the same boat Mary, he said.

They piled the luggage back again and the three of them retreated to the forest. No one could call it bush. The thin stream of insect sounds stilled for a moment. Her grandfather found a small patch of rough grass against a massive trunk, turned around several times, then collapsed against it like a sack emptying. Mary's mother sat bolt upright, her feet and knees together. She gazed upwards through the endless branches, searching for a sign.

A horn tooted. They peered out cautiously. A blue car had stopped. Sam leapt through the cocoon of dust from the front door to the boot, which he banged with his fist. The driver moved his right arm and the lid opened wide, a giant robot ready to disgorge. Sam pulled out the tyre and clutched it to him.

— He knows you, Grandad, he shouted.

The driver was a thin man with bent shoulders. He heaved himself out of the car, blowing air from rounded lips in tiny puffs. He steadied himself against the bonnet with a splayed hand of freckled fingers. His bald head was also freckled, half ringed with a fluff of faded ginger curls above the ears. His shirt hung loose, aglow with orange palms. Every movement of his body, including his smile, was slow.

— Long time no see then Lester, he said.

A bird lifted high above them.

— Listen, said Mary's grandfather. — Listen.

Rollo's Dairy (Jake and Deedee)

—He's good though isn't he? said Mrs Fussell.

Her puff cheeks creased as she smiled at the man sitting motionless in the cane chair beside the counter. She bent with a confiding creak until their faces were level.

— Yoo hoo Mr Rollo, she said.

Eyes blank as an empty screen, the man stared back at her.

— Hullo, he said.

— When you think of some of them, I mean. Mrs Fussell snapped upright as Jake punched the till with emphasis, moving slightly to avoid the shooting drawer.

— Yeah, he said. — Not bad for a hundred and ten.

— A hundred and . . . Oh, I'll tell Rex that one, promised Mrs Fussell. Chuckling with pleasure she hitched and slung her various carrier bags into position and teetered across the vinyl to the safety of the Have a Nice Day rug at the doorway.

— Of course Deedee's so lovely with him, she said.

Jake watched her as she stood beneath the old fashioned wooden awning of the dairy waiting for the lights to change. Even when the thing said Cross she still skittered about, nodding and bobbing her thanks to the tiger drivers clamped

BARBARA ANDERSON

behind their wheels. She was especially grateful to the tight-lipped women, their sleepy children, even, he felt, their enormous dogs. Jake had a sudden vision, so sharp, so ecstatically bright that he clutched the rim of the counter for a second. He saw himself tripping Mrs Fussell with a thrust of his leg, the left one, saw her spread-eagled on the crossing, flattened, her pink bloomers. He glanced down at the leg, blameless in walk shorts, socks, sandals, blew his breath out slowly and shook his head.

— Okay Pop? he said.

The man nodded.

— Okay Buster? he said to the child in the padded playpen. The baby lifted his arms. — Da da da, replied his son.

Jake made a joke about it once. Twenty-one years old. One wife. One Father gone gaga at fifty. One dairy. Two mortgages. One and a half kids. Where did I go wrong? Deedee loved it, curling up beside him on the lumpy sofa in the back room, her shape convex beneath her Live Cargo maternity shift, her mouth slightly open. She had read an exposé of sexism in International Airlines and learnt with interest that Asian air hostesses are instructed to part their lips slightly when attending to male passengers, as this is known to be both provocative and flattering. The article didn't say to whom, but Deedee rather liked the damp pouting look when she tried it out in the Coca Cola mirror above the sofa.

— It's because you couldn't resist me, she said.

Jake thrust his legs out in front of him then hooked one sandal across his knee and examined the sole. — Yeah, he said. Deedee laid her Sonata Gold rinse against his chest.

— Because I'm so beautiful, she said.

— Yeah.

— Why is it?

He placed two small stones on the glass topped table by his right arm and continued the examination of the sole

with the concentration of a mother chimpanzee grooming
her baby.
— Because you're so beautiful, he said.
— Stroke me, said Deedee, heaving herself onto her back.

Jake tried to work it out as they lay in bed together in
the room over the shop, Deedee's sweet breath puffing at
him occasionally across the giant pillow they shared. Why
have two. I like being close.
   She had always liked being close, ever since they had biked
to school together when she was in the third form. She
had none of the sharp-elbowed wariness of most of the
girls when confronted with the opposite species. Not that
she actually did anything the boys did, or nothing Jake could
remember, his eyes staring at the flicker from the neon
sign below the window.

There was a good hole in the Tuki Tuki that year, deep,
natural, no dam needed. They had fixed up a rope to the
willow, the usual thing, but that was the best year; a trunk
across a narrow inlet, a floating log, the lot. Deedee wouldn't
swim because of the slime. — Ooh ooh the feel of it, she
squealed, hands fanned across her face to shield the horror.
— And the smell! It did smell; a cloying green stench but
that was part of it, part of the whole thing and the heat
and the splashing shouts and the baked hay-like grass on
the banks. Each name familiar, carved till death. Names
echoed in those of the boys who nudged and elbowed at
the counter in front of him though there hadn't been a
Darryl like the new kid round the corner. Hem, Wayne,
Wayne had always been there, Grant, Mick, Shane, Kevin.
And Deedee, watching and applauding all of them, but
especially Jake. It got so he'd glance to check before he swung
wide on the rope.
   So she was his girl. As inevitable as growth, an extension,
one more thing Jake was good at. With his usual amiable
lack of effort Jake had the whole thing sewn up.

125

He was beautiful, his mother had always known this and wondered how it had happened, considering. A true North Country woman, she never admitted the fact even to herself. But when she was sure no one was looking she watched the grace of his hip-rolling walk, the light springing leaps as he ran upstairs. He was her only child. She always called him my son. Never ours.

She had met Jim Rollo when they were both working at the Wairakei hotel. She came from Leeds on a working holiday, waitressing on tables six to ten. Jim assisted in the golf pro's shop. He was a large man whose nobbly wrists shot from the sleeves of the long-sleeved shirts insisted on by the management. He was pleasant, that was the main thing about him, a nice man, especially compared with some of the more lecherous tourists. Her memories of fumbling courtship were filtered through dense clouds of steam from the Geothermal Bore.

They married and moved south to Hastings. Jim had hoped to buy a sports shop but the price was prohibitive — an arm and a leg, an arm and a leg. They settled for a dairy opposite the park where they worked from eight till seven, seven days a week, for seventeen years.

Jean Rollo's death shook the customers. — But she was so bright! they said. And so she was, bright, quick, attentive and clean. What more could they want. Her death destroyed Jim Rollo. — We were a team, son, he told Jake endlessly. It's like an arm gone. Or a head, thought Jake sadly, staring at the meticulous records of accounts and invoices in his mother's small neat writing.

She had never intended Jake to take over the dairy. With his beautiful body and his sport (summer and winter, Eleven, Fifteen), she saw him as a Physical Training Instructor. She had watched them once on a visit to Dunedin. The trainees were leaping a wooden horse in the grounds of the Training College. They warmed up in acid green track suits then discarded these on the icy benches so they could move even more easily in shorts and singlets. Jean Rollo watched them contract their bodies, tense themselves, spring into a run, a larger spring, up, over to drop down the other side light as cascading silk. She stayed staring for half an hour. A school first, she thought, then who knows, a university? Anywhere. Everyone wants them now. She had never told her plan to Jake. It was a secret to be revealed, like the acknowledgement of his beauty, when the moment allowed.

She died sliding to the floor one day beside the deep freeze, the sound of the packet of Stir Fry clattering to the ground Jim's first intimation of tragedy.

Jake went straight from school to help his father. He soon found he was running the place. Sighing deeply, his father glued himself to the sofa and the television in the back room. It wasn't Alzheimer's, the doctor insisted. — Then what is it? demanded Jake, begging for a name. — Nothing really ... I mean nothing with a long name, said Dr Francis, shambling about his surgery. — Here's his head, his heels are coming, Mrs Rollo used to say.

Dr Francis ran his practice with efficiency and compassion for his patients' pain. He knew better than most that many die young and fair but it was not for this reason that he longed to retire, to mooch endlessly after a golf ball accompanied by the distracted chatter of the sparrows in the macrocarpa shelter belts. — You know Dot, he had confessed to his wife that morning at breakfast, I'm so bloody sick of sick people.

— Nothing, said Dr Francis again. — He's just signed off.

— But he can't! stormed Jake.

— I'm afraid he can Jake, said the doctor.

Deedee was marvellous. She popped in to help with the orders every afternoon on her way home from school. It drove Jake insane when he heard his father explaining endlessly to her the finer points in the lives of the flickering figures on the screen. — That woman's a snorter Dee, he would say. — The one with the figure. She's trying to steal her own daughter's husband. Can you imagine any mother doing that? Jake heard through the red, black and yellow strips of plastic curtain his father's tooth-sucking contempt and Deedee's commiserating murmur. Once he couldn't stand it another minute. — Deedee! he shouted. — Where's the Mohlenbergs! The curtain slapped as she came running, placating, adorable. Why then did he feel she and his father were somehow . . . not together, that was insane. He didn't, he didn't, not with Deedee's hand slipping cool and intent beneath the belt of his walk shorts. — God, I love you, he said. — I know, said Deedee.

He could never have managed without her. He knew that. All the legal stuff. Power of attorney when it became essential, refinancing the mortgage, everything. How did she know so much? Not from her father, the useless clown. Nor from her mother, a gaunt silent woman who cleaned at the hospital. Her green uniformed figure biked with high lifting knees past the dairy twice a day. If she couldn't avoid it she lifted one hand to Jake, but normally she rode steadily, her eyes fixed straight ahead on the blue Kawekas in the morning, the cut out shape of The Peak on her return.

Deedee's kindness to the husk of Jim Rollo never faltered. It was all so weird. He could walk, dress, and feed himself. He had always taken care of his appearance and continued to do so, brushing his hair with those double hair brushes like the Duke of Windsor or something. He changed rooms with Jake soon after Jean died. — I can't stand it son, the double bed. His bedroom remained meticulously tidy, two *Golf* magazines placed neatly on the bedside table beside two *Autocars*. Nail scissors, tweezers, the brushes, were always in the same position on the tallboy. Behind them stood a small photograph of Jean taken twenty years ago. She looked like a little girl at her first party, her hair fluffed up around her face, her smile apprehensive.

Jake knew, not that he'd ever been told, that Wayne felt he'd been trapped into it by his wife Sheena. Jake had never felt that. He remembered the first time, when he and Deedee were still at school. She had opened her legs wide and welcomed him. Afterwards she sat up, dabbed her legs with her handkerchief, then rinsed it in the river with matter of fact composure. She beamed at him, her doll-sized cottontails in one hand as she brushed the grass from her bottom. She turned, standing on one leg as she pulled on her pants. The two cheeks matched with such breathcatching perfection that Jake fell on his knees, nuzzling. Deedee was shocked. — Jake! She smoothed her blue summer uniform and patted the crushed grass beside her. — Lie down, she said. Jake picked up a dead branch and heaved it at the Tuki Tuki. — Come on, said Deedee. — Lie down.

He was nineteen when they married, Deedee seventeen. She took over the ordering, running the reps with charm and steel. They all loved her, even Benchley in paper goods. He would slap his drooping corduroys, so different from the young guys' gear, and say, Deedee, I love you. The toughest teenage pro in the business.

Jason was born nine months later. Deedee loved being pregnant. Jake knew she would and was glad for her. He showed her a photo in *Woman's Own* of a pregnant film star sunbathing in a bikini. — That's like you, he said. — I don't sunbath in a bikini at nine months! — No, but you Luxuriate in Your Pregnancy, don't you? See. It says here. He stabbed his finger at the print. — Well, you're meant to. It's natural, isn't it? said Deedee, stumping through to the back room. — Hell yes, said Jake.

She had gone to the obstetrician for a routine examination. Jack was stacking the soups, tomato, vegetable, when the phone rang.

— This is Dr Petherton's surgery, said the crisp voice.

— What? said Jake.

— Dr Petherton has sent Mrs Rollo to hospital in an ambulance. The membrane has ruptured.

— What!

— Dr Petherton suggests you make arrangements to get

to the hospital right away, Mr Rollo. When Jake slammed the van into action he found he still had a Watties Tomato in his hand. He flung it across the seat and sat fuming at the red light.

Jason was born two hours later. Dr Petherton, half in love with all his golden girls, told Deedee she could make a fortune from a best seller entitled *How to Have a Baby*, by Alison Rollo. He said he'd be happy to write the foreword.

Deedee called the child Jason. — It's neat isn't it? Half yours and half mine. Aren't we lucky! she said scooping her left breast from the cross over top of her nightgown and fastening the button mouth around it as though this was another thing she had known for ever.

Why couldn't he revel in it all as she did? He knew you were meant to, knew how lucky he was. After the delivery he wanted to cry, to weep and weep and weep alone. Deedee was sweating, exhausted, beautiful in the joy of their shared gift.

— We could call him Alicob if we did it the other way, he said.

— Nutter, said Deedee proudly. He called the baby Ali for a while but the name didn't stick although it suited the child. He was a big baby. The down covering his large head changed to thick black curls, his skin was olive, his eyes dark, his expression dreamy. He was a solemn child, and seemed possessed of enormous indolence. Jake realised that babies normally were but he was puzzled by the fact that almost from the beginning Jason lolled at the breast with his eyes open. There seemed no attention to the matter in hand. — Shouldn't he shut his eyes or something? asked Jake. — Why? asked Deedee. Why indeed.

She was still feeding Jason at ten months when she found she was pregnant again.

— I think I'd better stop feeding him, she said sadly.

— Yeah, said Jake. — I reckon.

— I hate to do it. It seems so unfair, said Deedee, snatching Jason from his padded playpen and burying her head in

130

the nape of his neck.

The padded playpen-cum-cot was an unexpected and handsome present from Deedee's parents. It reminded Jake of a miniature boxing ring, just the shape of course. Every aspect of the thing was designed for comfort and protection. It was blue, the padded mattress base also blue with a scattering of bright yellow daisies. Deedee had attached various rattles and small fluffy toys around the rim. Jason lurched from one to the other chewing plastic rattles or miniature bears without discrimination, occasionally crashing backwards with a look of surprise on his smudged face.

— I think we should have the pen in the shop, said Deedee late one afternoon.

— Why?

— Well it's natural.

Jake felt the back of his neck prickle.

— I'll be in here more and more now he's older, Deedee explained. — Until you know, the baby.

— You'll hear him. If he wants you, he'll yell. You can go out. Jake stared at his son who was motoring around the playpen with more than usual speed.

Deedee turned to look at Jake, her face shocked.

— Don't you want him in the shop?

— Oh shit, Dee . . . Of course I want the little bugger.

— Jake!

The automatic buzzer sounded. Jake, who was leaning in the doorway to the back room, the giant liquorice straps of curtain streaming over his shoulders, leapt to the counter. It was only a packet of Rothmans but Jake greeted the defeated-looking man with enthusiasm.

— Certainly Sir. Just one was it? There y'go.

Deedee was sitting on the edge of the sofa when he returned, her eyes bright.

— I've already got Dad squatting there when he's not doing his Couch Potato act.

— What's that got to do with it?

— People won't like it, he tried.

— They will like it. They will. It's just what they will like, she insisted.

— You can't have the place cluttered up . . .

— Cluttered up!

They did like it. Jim Rollo they tolerated. Jason they loved.

Jake didn't take much notice of Darryl at first. He knew most of the kids in the area. Well not most, but a lot of them. Having grown up in the shop, seen them as babies, a combination of instinct and family histories advised him as to which ones to watch. All young kids pinch things, he knew that. He had himself, in Woolworths. They all did, with Deedee hovering at the door. He gave her a blue plastic hair slide he'd stolen, but she never wore it. They took anything which was easy, not necessarily because they wanted it. Once he pinched something when he didn't even know what it was. Deedee tried to snatch the pink elastic thing from him, her face scarlet. — That's awful. Awful! Give it to me. He caught the hot rush of shame. — It's for *girls*, she hissed. — I know that, but I thought it was a . . . — Give it to me! said Deedee shoving the thing in her school bag.

So he knew, as any dairy owner knows, to keep the glossy wrapped enticements of the Crunchies, Moros, Pinkies and Bounties behind him and the cigarettes in dispensers above his head. Only the spearmint leaves, wine gums, gobstoppers, milky chews — the kids' lollies — were displayed in their open boxes on the counter. He had stopped making up ten cent mixtures. He remembered himself. Half of it is the choosing. He was aware of the absence of some of the favourites of his childhood but arranged the survivors with care, keeping the boxes well filled so that his customers were not confronted by a few broken rejects beneath their sugar dust. — It's the little things that count, Deedee said, and Jake agreed. — Come and look, she said one Sunday. — Tom's made an effort with his weekend window. She took Jake's hand and led him to the butcher's shop next door. On a square of brown paper in the middle of the Snowline display cabinet stood two small black and white fibreglass pigs. One gazed straight ahead, bland and cheerful, the other, more suspicious, squinted upwards from beneath lowered brows. One non-biodegradable red rose lay between their tiny hooves, a wreath of white plastic daisies surrounded them.

— Isn't that neat. I like people who try. Like you, said Deedee, hugging his arm, her eyes on his.

— I better get back, said Jake. He opened another box of orange Jaffas and slipped it in the front row between the pallid sherbet lollies and milky chews for extra colour.

It wasn't only the kids who stole. He even had to chain the billboards to the front of the shop. A half-naked starlet you could understand, even Lady Di in a cowpat hat, but what sort of a wimp would want BROTHER CITED AS CO RE?

Darryl wasn't interested in the lollies or the billboards. He was a bright-looking kid, about nine or ten. Skinny, but boys are meant to be, with a wide grin. Whoever cut his tough blond hair had given up and cropped it close all over his head. He ignored Mr Rollo, but seemed pleased with the baby, whose playpen fitted neatly at the end of the canned goods row. Each time Darryl came to the shop he hunkered down to talk to Jason, encouraging him to undertake more daring playpen enterprises, extending one skinny finger through the bars as a prop. Jason beamed at him, a drool of saliva pouring down his chin. The boy picked up the spit rag and mopped.

— What's your name? Jake had asked, remembering how he'd hated being called son, or worse, sonny.

— Darryl. He clapped his hands at Jason, who hid his face on one knee in ecstasy.

— Got them at home, have you?

— Yeah.

He bought the usual things kids are sent to the shore for: bread, milk, the staples. He always waved to the baby before skidding off at a barefooted trot. — See y'.

— How long've you been here? Jake asked next time.

— Not long.

— Where d'you live?

The kid gestured with his head. — Round the corner. Credentials established, Darryl poked Jason in the stomach. Jason gazed at his stomach with solemn interest then got the idea. He seized the finger, placed it in his mouth and chewed.

— I think Darryl's lovely, said Deedee. — He's the only one of kids who really cares. Mopping up, I mean. That's lovely.

Jake lay staring at the dark, the flutter of neon visible through the gap in the curtains. He tossed onto his side, then checked to make sure he'd avoided pulling the lot with him, but Deedee was still covered. He lay very still. His head seemed to be growing larger and larger, a vast hollow space, expanding, filling the room, the street, the whole town. He gnawed the inside of his cheek, swallowed, but the sensation remained. He flung himself onto his back. It only seemed to happen when he lay sideways. Think of something. Think of something. He knew not to think about the shop. Figures muddled and jumbled in darkness became nightmares. He thought about Deedee, put out his hand to touch her. She murmured and rolled away. He thought of Jason and how he loved him. Of course he loved him but somehow he felt . . . not cheated, how could he? Why? How? Not because Deedee loved the baby and he felt left out. He'd read several articles about that too. Some were quite firm. 'Remember,' warned *Women*, 'to your partner, the father of your child, your son is another male animal.' Again Jake knew he'd got it wrong. His puzzled confusion was different. He had hoped the arrival of the baby would somehow lighten things. Take off some of the weight, not weight, there was no weight. But he had assumed that Jason's existence would dilute the essence, water down the concentrate of so much loving.

But Deedee's love, like energy from exercise, seemed self-engendering. The more she gave, the more she had. It flowed in endless draughts, more than enough for Rollo's three male animals and the entire world.

— Of course you're young, Mrs Fussell told him early next morning. — You and Deedee.

— You're bang on there, Mrs Fussell.

— But still it's long hours though, isn't it?

— Keeps us off the streets, Mrs Fussell. That's for sure. Jake slapped the useless piece of thin white paper around the half barracouta, sellotaped it, and put it in Mrs Bassett's spotless white cotton bread bag. Her pale eyes smiled at him. — I think you're just lovely, she said. — All of you. Her day enhanced by goodwill, she trotted off. Her small feet in their black cubans and white ankle socks reminded Jack of their counterparts next door.

He went straight to check the soups and meats. He didn't check every day, how could you, but just recently there was something odd. And the baked beans. He could have sworn the rows of beans plus sausages were level yesterday morning and he hadn't sold any. Deedee had been on while he did the banking, but he didn't want to mention it to her at this stage. He took a rough pad from the counter, made a count, then hid the sheet beneath the till. What could you do? You couldn't search bags. Not in a dairy for God's sake. That would be the kiss of death. Rage swept through him. One sodding thing after another. Inflation. GST. Every move they made seemed designed to destroy him. And now this.

He looked up. Darryl was watching him. Bare feet planted wide on the pink and green Have a Nice Day, he nodded at the empty playpen. — Jason not up yet? he asked.

135

— Doesn't look like it, said Jake. Darryl grinned. He always acknowledged jokes.

— What can I get you?

— I'll get it.

Darryl walked down the canned foods aisle, the vinyl bag banging against his knee scabs.

Jake stood very still. He put down his ballpoint, crept past the deep freeze, down the cereals and baking needs and peered around the corner into the canned goods aisle. Darryl's vinyl bag was collapsed on the floor. One hand held a tin. He bent and put the tin into his bag, the movement silent and furtive. Jake leapt at him, a flying tackle which brought them both crashing to the ground. The corned beef tin skidded down the aisle, several others rocked on their shelves. Jake leapt to his feet and slammed the terrified child hard against the shelves. Three more tins rolled crashing to the floor.

Jake's heart was belting in his chest. His hand tightened around the skinny neck. He could kill him, kill him! Darryl's hands clawed at the huge one, his face contorted. Shaking, sweating ice, Jake loosened his grip and clamped the boy's wrist. — Why! he shouted. — Why! Darryls' eyes were dilated, his breathing chaotic and rasping, the free hand clutched at his neck.

I nearly killed him. God, I nearly killed him. Jake leant against the soups, his hand still clamped around the bony wrist, breathing in, out, in, out. He forced himself to look at the thief.

— Look, he said. — Look. This is my stuff! I work for it. I slave my guts out. His fury engulfed the glistening face. — I don't come to your place and pinch your stuff.

— We haven't got any stuff, whispered Darryl.

Jake exploded, his arms windmilling, legs flaying. — Get out of here! Get out of here, y'little shit. Get out!

Darryl fled. Jake picked up the vinyl bag and thundered up the aisle, snatching the corned beef as he ran. Darryl skidded on the mat, crashed to the ground, picked himself

up and lurched out the door. Jake leapt onto the empty
early morning pavement and heaved the bag and the tin
after the fleeing boy. Darryl paused for a second, then, still
bent double, retrieved them both and disappeared around
the corner.

Jake leant against the end of the aisle, his heart thumping.
He wiped the back of his hand across his eyes. From the
blur beneath his eyes spiky yellow shapes defined
themselves. He stared as the familiar shapes of the playpen,
the straight sides, the soft padded curves of the mattress,
the chewed bears, surfaced into focus as though pushed
from beneath.

— Oh Christ, he whispered. — Sweet Christ.

It is Necessary I Have a Balloon

— Well, it is my birthday, Tom said, leaning back against the heaped pillows, hers as well as his cushioning his back.

— I know. She continued folding the crumpled wrapping papers, aligning the sides with care, creasing the fold with thumb and forefinger, flattening the useless stuff against her jeans with brisk sweeping movements of her hand.

— Why do you do it!

— What? She glanced up, her face half covered by the huge fashionable glasses.

— Save the paper. He smiled. — You look like an owl, he said. — A Small Barn Owl.

She jumped up. His hand steadied the sliding mug as the tray bucked. She stood the cards upright on the chest of drawers. One had a rod and fishing gear draped around *Happy birthday, Dad*. Chosen with tongue-biting care for a non-fisherman by his daughters from the selection labelled Male. From depictions largely of manly pleasures, veteran cars, racehorses, balls, bats, pads, she had chosen a noble-headed lion. Its expression of benign autocracy was enhanced by a magnificent mane. Its eyes were kind. Under the inscription, 'A birthday card for you today, to say you're loved in every way,' she had written, 'Kind regards, Jan.' The joke had flopped.

He tried again. — So what about it?

She scooped the washing from the floor and clutched it lovingly to her chest. — Well it's just the kids, she said, wriggling a free hand in attempted clarification. — You know, your birthday . . . She thought of the plump and gleaming chicken, the paper hats, the stricken faces.

— That's right! It's my birthday. Why d'y' think I skipped the wine tasting? And the dinner? His voice sharpened at the memory of his sacrifice. He saw Grant oiling alongside the man from Sydney as he left. Saw himself crouched in a purple bucket seat among the graveyard faces waiting for the last plane, the only energy that of two toddlers in red parkas who hurtled around snatched at by a distracted woman with spiked hair. The flight had been bumpy, the air hostess's farewell smile a rictus.

He took another swig of cold coffee from his birthday mug, replaced it, and put the tray carefully on her side of the bed. He kicked the duvet back with both feet, padded to the door and turned. His head lifted. She was reminded of the lion.

— I just want to go to the Molloy's party.

And so you shall Cinderella. But she was puzzled.

— Why do you want to? So much I mean.

He scratched his left buttock and yawned. — Carol'll be there. You know, Anna's sister. I want to dance with her.

— Why particularly?

— Because, he said, she dances with animal grace.

— Animal *what*?

— Grace, he said, his bare feet slapping the stained floor as he moved to the bathroom.

— It's Dad's birthday you see . . .

— We know *that*, said Rita, her round face stern.

— Yes well you see he wants to go to this party and we'll have his party here tomorrow night.

— Why? Implacable, squat as a lunch box in her yellow

dungarees, tow hair bunched at right angles, Rita was unconvinced.

— Because he wants to dance with this lady.

— Oh for Christ's sake, he groaned from behind the *Herald*.

She swung at him, her arms stiff with outrage. — Well *you* get out of it!

He leant back and slapped the paper over his face.

— I can danth, said Jessie. She hefted her frock over the solid curve of her belly and stumped about shaking her bottom.

— So can I! Rita the ever competitive swung herself into the phantom beat.

— So can I! shouted their mother. They rocked and swayed and lurched about, enchanted with themselves and their dance.

— Give me strength! He flung his Docksides on the sofa to lie full length, his face hidden by news.

The balloons jerked everyone's eyes upwards. The Molloy's high-raked ceiling was awash with them. They clung in the steep angle of the beamed roof as though magnetised, their boiled-sweet skins ovoid and tight. Each had a streamer attached which drifted languidly in the currents and streams of talk, the shrieks of joy.

— Helium! cried Jan. She knew.

— Where did you get it? Tom asked Anna Molloy.

Anna's hair was sweet disorder, her mind racing. How had she got into this. Self inflicted wounds. Open the door. Go home, go home, go away.

— Industrial Gases, she screamed, handing Jan and Tom's coats on to ten-year-old Rob. Good God the Balfours. She swept to embrace them.

Rob's round-eyed gaze was solemn. — Dad knows a guy, he told them, hanging their coats with responsible care.

Jan's hair was falling down. She shifted her weight onto her other foot and gazed into the eyes of the man talking to her. She hadn't heard his name. His rust-coloured shirt was faintly pharmaceutical in design. It buttoned off centre, his neck rising from a stand up collar. If her chemist dyed his uniform in Cold Water Dylon he too could have one.

He dropped his eyes. They were blue; so strong a blue that if you saw him across a cafeteria you would think, That man has blue eyes.

— Well you did ask, he said.

— Yes, she said, wondering what.

His glance flicked down again. — Where are your shoes?

— I didn't want to come.

— Oh. The pause was too long. — I'll get you a drink.

— I'll get it, she said, but he was gone.

She turned to the anxious woman beside her.

— Balloon's are great, aren't they Margie?

Margie's eyes searched the room, checking each corner for secrets. Her lipstick was weeping, leaving sad imprints on the cold glass. — Nnn, she said. — Lovely party.

The noise level was increasing, the balloons drifting tails moved more rapidly in the warmer air. The room was full of people who cared about issues and were beautiful.

Tom stood by the door with Carol, his body canted in the drooping curve of a tall man talking to a small woman.

— Your husband's so good-looking, said Margie.

— Tom? Yes. Has been for some time.

A thousand years. Where was that rust-coloured clown?

Excusing herself to Margie, who looked as though she might howl at this defection, she slipped on her shoes and moved away.

The bar was a mess, sloppy and disorganised. Giant bottles of spirits stood in puddles, soft drinks were muddled beside used glasses. Cardboard wine flasks gushed and flowed. She tried to back out but was trapped in the crush of supplicants.

— Wine please, she said to the sweating boy whose T-shirt shouted obscenities at her. Holding her glass like a chalice she slid off at one side of the bar table. Someone turned on the stereo. *Flash Dance* surged and racketed around her.

People began to dance. Tom was quite right. Carol moved as though she was born for nothing else; her hair swung, her eyes were dreamy, her mouth slightly open.

Perhaps she could do something? Toss a salad? Hell bent on salad tossing, clutching a sticky glass, Jan stood staring at Carol and the balloons.

She moved from the living room to the passage. There were no balloons here. She missed their colour, their lazy completeness.

She trailed along the passage, opening doors. The master bedroom was pink. There was no evidence of Michael Molloy other than *Time* and a digital clock on the left hand table. Full-blown roses crawled across the double bed, mushroom pink lay wall-to-wall, pink ribbons ruched and fell from the lampshades.

Backing out quickly, Jan tried another door.

— Hang on! a voice cried.

Irritated, she retreated back up the herring-gutted hall. The sounds of the party swirled and stamped beyond the thin wall.

The kitchen door opened at her touch. Against the huge refrigerator Carol was flattened. Only the top of her head above Tom's shoulder was visible, and a drift of green polyester trapped behind his moleskins.

The door shut automatically as she blundered backwards. She clutched the arm of a man ambling along the passage from the bathroom.

— I want a drink.

— So do I. Wait here.

She stood staring, hypnotised by the row of coats. Each peg had at least six coats hanging from it. Some had fallen to the ground. She aimed a kick at Tom's tartan-lined raincoat but moved her foot quickly as the man reappeared.

— I've found a bottle and glasses, he said. — Do you drink whisky?

— Anything. Don't go in there.

— Why not?

— Yes, she said. — Why shouldn't you?

He looked at her.

— I've gone off the idea, he said. — But we need some water.

— Here. She opened the door next to the kitchen.

— Ah, he said, peering at the whiteware. He placed the open bottle on the window sill, then poured two drinks, adding water from the cold water tap above the tub.

— Here's to our side.

— Thank you.

— To hell with stomp and grind.

— Yes. She paused, the glass half way to her lips. — Excuse me, she said moving to the door.

— Where're you going?

— I'm going to chuck it at someone.

His face was shocked, his grasp on her wrist a manacle. — No, he said. — Not whisky.

She put the glass on the windowsill and turned to fight him. Average height, glasses, a thatch of black hair, a face that looked as though someone had pulled all the lines downwards, dragging fingers through plasticine.

Her shoulders shrugged. — O.K. she said.

— What's your name? he asked, releasing her wrist.

— It doesn't matter.

— I don't suppose it does. No. Let's make ourselves comfortable.

He opened the clothes dryer and groped in its black hole. His hand appeared holding a blush-pink duvet which he doubled and spread on the floor.

— What a bit of luck. Good old Baby Doll Molloy.

They slid down onto its softness, then leant against the cool comfort of the Fisher and Paykel, the whisky bottle

143

between his outstretched legs, a faint whiff of soap powder in the air.

— You're in such a strong position with your own bottle.

— Yes, she said.

Shoulder to shoulder they sipped their drinks.

The kitchen door clunked open, pushed from inside.

— Thank you, Tom, sang Carol, If you'd just bring the salami.

Jan choked on her gulp of whisky. Shoulders heaving, eyes streaming, she snorted the stuff from her nose.

— I'm sorry . . . It's just . . . It's just . . . she panted.

Steadying the whisky bottle with one hand, he reached out and pulled her back so that her head lay on his shoulder. His arm slipped around her.

— It's all right, he crooned. — It's all right.

Her hiccough was doubtful but she lay back. — I like whisky, she said.

— Hang on. He freed his arm, moved the bottle, then removed his glasses and turned towards her again. — It'd be like antlers clashing, he said.

Eventually she pulled away from him. Her eyes stung with rage.

— Do you know what a glottal stop is? she said quickly.

— No, he said.

— It's in a book I'm reading. She keeps talking about glottal stops.

— Look it up.

— I can't be bothered.

Breathless at such wit, they sank lower on the blush pink, their arms entwined, the whisky bottle safely on one side. The beat of rock music pulsed through the walls and the floor beneath them.

— I can feel it in my bum, he said, pleased.

— Do you ever go to Kentucky Fried? she asked later, enunciating with care.

— Of course, he said.

144

— Who goes in and gets it?

— Hunh?

— You or your wife?

— Oh. He considered, his face more creased than ever.
— I haven't a wife at the moment. But I used to. Get it
I mean.

She snuggled down on the duvet.

— Nice, she murmured.

— Come home with me, he said.

She shook her head and sat up, then rolled forward and
clambered up. She heaved her skirt down, supporting herself
against the gleaming washing machine. She observed the
scene from a great height. He lay far below, crumpled, boozy,
friendly, clutching his half-empty bottle, cradled in pink.

— No. I'm going home.

She bent down, kissed his glistening forehead, then
stepped carefully over the wreck of his trouser legs and
walked the few steps to the door.

His attempt to clutch her ankle was half-hearted. She
turned and lifted a hand to him, then closed the door. The
party racketed on, rock music thundered over the heads
of the dancers, the eaters, the drinkers.

Her hair had collapsed completely, her glasses were
crooked. She picked her way with care through the throng,
very polite, very cautious as the dancers stamped and swayed
about her. — I want a balloon, she told them. She reached
the opposite wall and tugged a small table into position,
then skirted the room and returned smiling with a small
chair from the hall which she placed in the exact middle
of the table. She kicked off her shoes, hitched her tight
skirt up over her thighs and clambered onto the table, then
teetered tiptoe on the fragile chair, her arm stretched
upwards grasping for a balloon. The noise was louder still
at ceiling level. Tom's head jerked upwards from the
stomping haze below. — I want a balloon, she told the
uplifted sweating face, the stunned mullet mouth. — It is
necessary I have a balloon.

145

Subalpine Meadow

It beats in my head so I hear it although there is no sound. It doesn't match the rhythm of my painting hand. You'd think there would be a sweeping 'Dah, da DAH, da da da' sequence as I broad brush the mountains. Not the bounce and stump of 'One O'Clock, Two O'Clock, Three O'Clock ROCK', a tune which slots me in my slice of time. I am a child of the fifties.

I live with my mother and have no man to speak of, which seems an odd way of putting it. My mother's grace belies her age, I've been told. She has very little bust, but she is undeterred. She stuffs tissue paper down where it would be if it were larger, though lately she has given this up and who can blame her. Presumably she had more originally, it's not a thing we have ever discussed. It hasn't cropped up. I was amazed when I read that Julie Nixon was amazed that 'as a family we never discussed Watergate'. What did she expect?

My mother drifts through life. Moving languidly she trails through the days. Floating diaphanous fabrics, scarves, shawls and ribbons attend her. In the wind they get out of control and have to be constrained. Today she is swathed in beauty like a Byzantine Madonna. Long nosed, dark eyed, she appears on the back porch and clutches the wooden ball on the top of the newel post for support.

— What on earth do you think you're *doing* Kate! she screams.

I have been expecting this. I am cool. Cool.

— Painting the fence, I call merrily. Merrily, merrily shall I live now.

— Mad as a hatter, moans my mother.

I flick an upward curve to the stiff leaf of my Mountain Daisy. I have transformed the dull blue fence at the back of the section into a Subalpine Herbfield or Meadow, of daisies. Beneath the zigzag peaks of mountains their white slashes of petals spring from rosettes of flat leaves, or are glimpsed among tall spiky ones, easy to paint with a medium brush in St. Albans. I dream of the mountains. All the time. The daisies march half way across the fence. I wipe the brush on newspaper and stow it in a jam jar of turps before turning to my mother.

— Don't you like it? I ask.

I work at a sub-branch of a Diagnostic Laboratory out at Woolston. We all said we'd leave when they moved out there, but none of us did. A rottweiler tied by a running chain to the clothesline next door barks its heart out in endless despair. The Lab is housed in a former state house which they must have got cheap. It is surrounded by repeating images of itself which melt to the horizon. In rooms designed to protect, possibly even comfort, we spin urine in centrifuges, we count blood cells, we stain sputa.

I have been with the firm for ever. Unqualified, but good at it, I am regarded as a fixture less exciting than the new microscope, but more reliable than the centrifuge.

On Monday Geoffrey our Senior is angry again. His shoulders hunched over the microscope reject us all, even Trudy. His beautiful head may be contemplated, the deep waves in his hair noted as they sweep back to tight curls at the nape of his neck. He probably doesn't know they exist and I have no words to tell him.

— You must've seen it on the direct slide, Trudy, he says at last.

— No, says Trudy our Junior. She unwinds one leg from around the other and places her shoes neatly together, toes straight ahead. She regards their pointed ends with affection, bending from her neat little bottom to get a better view.

Geoffrey swings around on his stool, snatching his spectacles from the bench. He looks so vulnerable, uncooked almost without them, I have to turn away till he has regrouped.

— Trudy it's not good enough, he says. He stands and leans over her, willing her, forcing her to understand the meticulous care required, the exact observation, medical ethics even.

— The plate's grown a heavy pure culture. Surely you must've seen *something* in the direct slide? he begs.

Her smile is a mirror reflecting unwanted junk.

— I just didn't I guess, says Trudy. Last week when Trudy misread a plate I explained her error tactfully. She looked at me kindly, the whites of her eyes blue as well.

— So? she said.

Elaine in haematology is a horse of a different colour, a dark horse. Hunted, haunted, divorced, could have been the boss but isn't, she works meticulously and very very slowly. Nothing disturbs her monumental disregard for the crises which occur daily, her refusal to accept one teaspoon of responsibility for which she has not been paid.

Elaine's hair is beautiful also. She sweeps it onto the top of her head, like a woman in an old photograph whose hand rests on the back of a chair on which a man sits encased in Edwardian trousers. Elaine is slim, her hair is the colour of ripe wheat, and if you've ever seen that you will know it is not gold, more a sunny fawn. Pieces escape from Elaine's bun so that she moves in an aura of floating wisps, as does my mother although different. Elaine's eating method has more appeal than most; it is as though she is unaware of her sandwich or pie until a piece has been bitten off and stored within her mouth for mastication purposes. Elaine does not tuck in. She *transfers* food, almost unknowingly. In this she resembles many fat women — but their seeming unawareness of food disposal is simulated, and stems from a different cause.

Harry, our Intermediate, does tuck in. He motors through food, and in fact life. His enthusiasm is at the ready like a towel at a waiter's waistband. He is not much older than Trudy, but he cares about the work very deeply. His tough brown curls leap from his bullet head, his step is quick as he moves with anticipation to the incubator each morning to get the culture plates.

— Come along gang, he cries in his Ricardo voice. — We are not here to make frenz.

Ricardo is our other staff member. He is the storeman, caretaker, the one who sterilises the rubbish in the autoclaves and bags it up. He comes from Venice; his English is not perfect like ours, so we laugh at it, and by extension, at him. This is harmless as we have nothing against Ric, nothing at all. We like him in fact, his neat movements as he tugs the stores about the shed, his lopsided smile as he greets us. — Good zay. I like him a lot.

But the Laboratory is not a Happy Ship. Hardly anyone likes anyone else too much. Harry despises Trudy. — Heavy scene in the tearoom, Kate, he tells me at the end of the week. — Ah, I say. — Trudy threw a wobbly. — Not again? — Yeah. He swings around on his stool and aims a phantom .45 at me.

— Don't rap with the fuzz, kid, he warns, now in his Al Capone mode. He means don't tell the Boss in Town the Intermediate at Woolston has reason to believe the Senior is having it off with the Junior.

— Negative, I say, slipping another slide under my microscope.

149

My mother indicates the tangle of neglected garden as evidence that it's not as though the whole place isn't crying out. She then gives up on the fence. Having made her protest she withdraws in sighing disapproval. She gave up some time ago on my clothes. She is perhaps glad of signs of increasing eccentricity on the part of her daughter. It makes her more interesting, a fragile threatened creature trapped with some sort of familial nutter. I imagine her in the living room where she plays compulsive bridge. The curtains are drawn as the colours may fade, the chintzes are the deep purples, roses and buffs of corals bunched beneath shadowed seas. She tells Amy, Beryl and Con. — Sometimes I wonder about Kate. I mean seriously. But the Girls will reassure her, touching their lacquer for comfort. — Oh Kate's all right, they will tell my mother. — Don't worry about Kate.

Things are coming to a head in Woolston. The Laboratory situation approaches critical mass as Geoffrey is torn between his duty to sack Trudy and his need to cup her pretty buttocks in his large grateful hands. After her last serious error his eyes blinked tears, and even Trudy was not blithe. Harry steams in righteous disgust.

— Calls himself the Boss out here, he mutters. — Why can't he be a man? he asks, and sack the bitch?

But Geoffrey is, but Geoffrey is, and his hands hang empty with grief.

The rottweiler's agony is getting to us also. It now howls. We ring Noise Abatement, we whinge in sympathy with the dog's misery.

Elaine withdraws further, counting blood corpuscles at glacial speed. Ric remains cheerful. Dusty but calm he cleans out the storeroom. Hissing between his teeth as though grooming a horse, he stacks cartons of agar in segregated piles. He knows that this order, this clarity of intent, will not survive the daily scramble but does it anyway.

As the tension defuser, the one who can work with

everyone, I become over-merry. Harry and I sing our Weepy.
— Hush, not a word to Geoffrey, we moan. — He might
not *understand*. Geoffrey does not smile, but Ric does. Like
the deaf, the disregarded, or uncomprehending, he smiles
often. When anyone laughs he smiles to indicate that he
has not missed the joke. He smiles as he goes about his
work. Some people in wheelchairs do this too. It is a signal,
the opposite of Mayday.

Ric is good with the autoclaves. The snorting, belching
things can be tricky.

— This one isn't constant at fifteen, Ric, I tell him one
morning as I go to collect the fresh culture plates.

— Juz a lil juzzment, he replies and makes it.

— Tell me about Venice, Ric, I say.

— Your Venice is not my Venice, he says.

— I haven't got a Venice.

— You will one day. One day you go and you come back
and you will say Ah Venice and everyone will say Ah Venice
and you will not see the filth and the stink and hunger
even. Venice! Take up it the ass!

I am enchanted. — Ric, I'm *mad* about you!

— Shuddup, he says. There is a pause as he heaves the
tray of rubbish out of the autoclave. Steam pours out, as
from a loco in an old movie. Ric dumps the tray and turns
to me, still in his heavy gloves. — Why do you do it, like?
he asks. — The rubber bands?

— Hunh? My hair hangs either side of my face,
Pocahontas with rubber bands.

— Oh. To keep it out of the way. The specimens.

— One real good thing in Venice is Titian, he says.

— Your hair is Titian. He slams the autoclave door. —
Rubber bands! I pick up the tray of plates and depart.

Despite my impatience to share the Venice one with
Harry, I wait till we have finished planting out the swabs,
as we both care and are good workers and don't chat on
the bench. I don't begin until the cultures are in the incubator
and the urines swinging in the centrifuge.

151

— One day you go and you come back and you will say Ah Venice and you will not see . . .

I am in good form. My mimicry is exact. Harry and Trudy are laughing so hard their fillings show, even Elaine smiles weakly before turning back to her unending thankless task.

— Take up it ze . . .

— Shuddup! shouts Ric from the doorway, his face bleached, his hands shaking. I fall off my high stool.

— Ric . . . I start.

— Shuddup! he spits at me again. My shame is a dumper wave knocking me breathless. Ric slams the door and I am lost.

He still won't look at me. He cannot see me. I am the other side of the moon in darkness. The hissings and mutterings, the curses and bitches of laboratory unrest continue but I don't hear, don't care, don't jolly anyone, not even Harry. — Stuff them, I think, as though it is someone else's fault I have betrayed my friend, and surely that is too strong a word and what does it matter. My Subalpine Meadow is no help. It no longer spins me into a mountain dream as I sit on the bus. Maybe I'll finish it this weekend and then it will be finished and so what. Will I even look at it much? — Forget it, forget it, forget it, I tell myself not meaning the fence, but the mind is its own bouncer and a tough one at that, and won't admit even vacant harmless amnesia without a pass.

I don't finish the fence. I hardly look at it and my mother says — Well are you going to finish it or not? and I say — I don't know, and she says — Merciful heaven, and glides to the telephone which is her lifeline to normal people who swim in her world.

I sit in the bus on Monday morning thinking of nothing. I watch two small boys across the aisle who are engrossed in conversation. One is very serious; he confides and explains at earnest length. The other shakes his spiky hedgehog head

152

and laughs. He does not believe, will never believe, that life is anything but a laughing joke.

There are no cars outside the Lab, only Ric's pick-up truck. I stump up one of the concrete strips of the drive, my thighs bouncing against each other. Three standard roses left by some previous owner struggle towards extinction. I push open the door and am astounded. The Laboratory has disappeared. I mean completely. The walls, the benches have been stripped, there are no stools, no microscopes, no bench racks, nothing. Nothing remains, not even the incubator or the centrifuge. The walls have been painted Arctic White, everything has been painted. There are no people. The ceilings, the walls, the window sills shimmer back at the emptiness.

I turn to see Ric staring at me from the doorway.

— What's happened? I gasp.

He is not impressed. — It's been painted, he says.

— But but . . . ? I start laughing. I drop my shoulder bag, my knees buckle as I weave around the room laughing.

— Nobody, nobody, nobody, I gasp.

— Didn't they tell you? On Friday?

— No, no, nobody. Nobody. I will never speak again. Laughter is the only thing. Laughter and oblivion.

— What a pack of bums, says Ric. Then he begins to laugh. Moving with the stately care of the very drunk, clutching the bench at intervals, we laugh and laugh and laugh.

Eventually Ric moans. — They had to tell me for the humping. Only the humping. We continue the gut-wrenching catharsis of the untold, we beam at each other in the empathy of the excluded. Tears of joy spout from our eyes, we clutch each other. — No one, I pant. — Not one of the bastards.

— I'll give you a lift home, he says. — It's shut till tomorrow. All the day shut. I've got to put the stuff back.

I crawl upright from my bench. — I'll show you my fence, I say.

BARBARA ANDERSON

My mother is playing bridge at the Club. Shy as any Artist
at an Opening, I lead the way around to the back, brushing
past the papery hydrangea heads. Ric follows in silence.
When I see the fence with his eyes I am seven years old
and not happy. Still staring at it he takes the brush from
the jar at the back steps, wipes it on the turpy rag, then
sticks the handle in the back pocket of his jeans. He skips
the lid from the tin of white paint with a screw driver,
stirs it with the stick beside it, then moves down the rough
grass springing from the soles of his beat up Adidas like
a slow motion dancer on TV, the brush in one hand, paint
pot in the other.
— Don't! I panic. — You don't know. How can he know?

It's all right. Mountain daisies sprout from his brush, his
hand is sure, the white petals spike out. His strokes get
faster, daisies leap across the fence, in clusters, alone, or
in drifts that multiply.
I open my two green pots, grey-green and a small bright
glossy, give them a quick stir, grab the brushes and am
in business. Our brushes stub and sweep the fence.
— Middles. Their middles, says Ric. — Get the yellow.
Its my fence. And I'm busy.
— You get it, I say.
Ric flings back his head to laugh.
— O.K. he says, and gets it.

154

School Story

The story begins in the staff room.

Miss Franklin has her knife deeper than ever into Miss Tamp. She has already flattened her over detentions, and she has not given an inch on parent participation which is a controversial topic in need of discussion.

Several staff members don't know where to put themselves. The blue, brown, brown eyes of Ms Powdrell, Ms Murchison and Ms Doyle (Sooze, Margot and Carmen) are wide with spectator interest. They are young. They climb up mountains and into deep valleys out of which they must scramble as best they can, their hearts bumping and their hands full. Our less experienced staff members Miss Tamp calls them. Shit, think Carmen, Margot, and Sooze, and Carmen's mind adds that Miss Tamp should sack the bitch. Who's Head anyway? Margot and Sooze, however, admire Miss Franklin because she is an excellent teacher and has iron control even in 4F though of course it is not called that now. Still even so, shit, they think. They see the handle between the shoulder blades and watch the blood drip dripping as in *Tess of the D'Urbervilles*. Margot's shoulders move in unconscious sympathy, Sooze wriggles lower in her plastic chair. Carmen lights a cigarette in the staff room smoke-free zone and dares Miss Franklin with her young eyes.

— Put it out, says Miss Franklin without a please and Carmen leaves the table, her long plait leaping from side to side across her back with the impetus of her departure. Carmen is Phys Ed and smokes very rarely. Mr Tysler smiles.

The older members have seen it all before, but even so. Mrs Toon (Maths) gazes at the ceiling, her verruca is giving her gyp and she can't remember if she has another tin of Gourmet Beef and Heart in the cupboard above the sink. She tries to visualise the contents of the cupboard, her mind moving over the gaily labelled soups to the flat Herrings in Tomato Sauce to the small oval-shaped tin of anchovies left over from the time when she made her own pizzas and her youngest asked if those fish were sad. She thinks she has another Gourmet but it is better to be safe than sorry. Mrs Toon will stop off at the dairy.

Mr Tysler is Art and fed up. His face is rugged country. His beard is untracked bush. His body moves continuously, his legs writhe in a kinetic sculpture of frustrated boredom. His hands tap the table, his feet scrub the carpet squares. He hates Miss Franklin, he despises Miss Tamp. He has had it up to here with sodding kids and sodding females though he fantasises about Carmen. He aches for her as she flounces back to the table having finished her cigarette gesture and flops down muttering Sorry to Miss Tamp who doesn't know what to do. Miss Franklin knows exactly what to do. Carmen smiles back at the glare across the table. Her hands are folded in her lap. Her plait is still. She is a good girl again. Mr Tysler lifts his hands from the table and slams them between his thighs. He could weep. And weep.

— Can't we get *on*, he mutters.

The other more experienced staff members including Miss Hobbs, Mrs Benchley, Mrs Hopere, Mrs Medgley and the part-timers indicate their agreement. They nod, smile, scrape their chairs, sigh, look at their watches, shuffle papers, scratch about in their carrier bags, stare at the ceiling, bite the insides of their mouths, scratch about in carrier bags and clamp their lips tight as they role-play their role as a captive audience. Mrs Stillburn continues her abstract doodle. She adds a circle to the point of the middle pyramid, encloses this within another pyramid then shades in with quick decisive strokes of her Air New Zealand ballpoint. Mr Tysler has his head in his hands.

Miss Tamp has resumed command. Her face is stern, her complexion blotched red on white.

— Yes indeed, yes *indeed*, she says.

Ms Jenni Murphy who is vegan has discovered a small jar of bean sprouts hidden beneath papers in the bottom of her kete. She takes out the jar and inspects it with interest, shakes it, peers at it, then puts it back having resisted the temptation to take off the lid and have a good sniff as she would like to. She didn't know she had it she whispers to Mr Tysler who does not reply.

— Now the final item, says Miss Tamp. — Gowns at Prizegiving.

Gowns, writes the Head's secretary, Mrs Sinclair. She thanks God that she made the curry last night. The thought of not having to start from scratch is so comforting that she smiles.

Miss Tamp smiles back.

— Gowns at Prizegiving repeats Miss Tamp. — Several members of the staff, she says, glancing at the younger members, don't own gowns. Carmen returns a vigorous nod of encouragement. — They cost the earth she murmurs with downcast eyes. Margot and Sooze don't know where they are. Their smiles are non-commital. — So therefore, continues Miss Tamp speaking rather fast, I have decided that gowns will not be worn at Prizegiving.

Miss Franklin's voice slices out from an ice cave. — The last shred of dignity gone from what used in Miss Sargesson's time, to be a memorable occasion, she says.

— Jesus wept mutters Mr Tysler. Miss Franklin bounces round to face him. There is uproar at the staff meeting. There is agreement, disagreement, frustration, rage, aching

157

BARBARA ANDERSON

boredom and a trickle of anarchy. Hands slam the table.
A part-timer's chair topples as she leaps up. She is off. She
has had it up to here. Her neighbour Mrs Sinclair lays a
restraining hand on the day-glo track suit and whispers.
The part-timer rights the chair and crashes back onto it
muttering. Carmen reaches for her cigarette packet which
she has left sitting with a Bic lighter on the table. — Ladies!
Ladies! cries Miss Tamp.

Mrs Benchley (English) straightens her back. — Things
have changed since Miss Sargesson's time, she says, brushing
the front of her shell pattern with quick downward flicks
of her right hand.

Miss Franklin bounces from Mr Tysler. Her hair is a white
crest. Her hands clamp the table to hide their shaking.

— What do you mean!

Mrs Benchley is almost satisfied with her front. She picks
a final fleck of white off and lifts her head to Miss Franklin's
eyes. — Just that she was a thousand years behind the times,
she says.

— If you consider . . . ! But Miss Franklin's rage has
trapped her subtle words. They cannot get out to fight.
Mrs Benchley consolidates.

— The place was pickled in aspic she says. There are
puerile sniggers of laughter. Miss Tamp's head swings from
side to side. She is a trapped umpire.

Miss Franklin is on her feet, her hands reach out as she
leans across the table to kill Mrs Benchley.

Miss Tamp resumes control. — Ladies! Ladies! she cries.

Now Mr Tysler's chair topples. The less experienced
members of staff clutch themselves with delight as he storms
from the room swinging his canvas bag up onto his shoulder
in an enraged sweeping arc.

It is morning break next day. Sooze lifts her head from
The Population Explosion.

— What've you got on? she asks Margot.

The yellow plastic spoon in Margot's hand is stilled. Her

face is anxious. — Is it too strong? she asks.

It is but never mind. Sooze shrugs. — What is it?

— Stephanotis. Margot dips her head quickly to her shoulder and sniffs, testing for overkill. She sits on the large table between two piles of marking. Her soft red lace-up boots are on the seat of a plastic chair.

— I hate scent at work says Carmen. She tips her chair back. — What about last *night* though! She says.

Margot agrees with Sooze and Carmen that the whole thing was over the top. She adds that she liked Alec not being able to handle being called a lady for God's sake.

— Did you see his face!

— No one can see his face, says Sooze.

Margot continues shovelling shell-shaped pasta salad into her mouth with the yellow spoon. She is selective, she removes small pieces of chopped onion which she places on the lid of the container for later disposal. The pasta is decorated with cubes of red and green peppers but it still does not appeal to Sooze.

— Yuk, she says.

— He's not that bad, mumbles Margot. Sooze does not bother to explain as she doesn't have to eat it and she is now searching the numerous pockets of her stone-washed denim skirt. She knows she has a bus ticket somewhere which she wishes to use as a bookmark. She finds the small useful thing and is reassured.

— What we're talking about here, says Carmen, is a confrontation situation. The faintest shadow of golden hair is visible above her upper lip as she swings around to the window to touch a bud of the gift-wrapped cyclamen plant on the window sill. Mrs Sinclair had to dash out during her lunch hour yesterday because she had forgotten her aunt's birthday and then forgot to take it home but she has explained to Aunt. The puce buds hang like toy furled umbrellas, a green calyx frill at each throat. Aunt will be pleased thinks Carmen.

— Anyone who can control 4F, well whatever they are

now, has my vote, says Sooze. She sees the rows of sullen faces, senses her failure, her occasional prickle of fear. What can she do. — It's not your fault, her lover tells her as she lies confiding in his arms each night. — It's not theirs, says Sooze. This she knows. She had thought this knowledge would save her. Sometimes Bryce feels as though he works at Girls' High all bloody night. He is getting hacked off. No one told Sooze teaching would be war. If they had she would not have believed them. Sooze is a good teacher, she knows she is a good teacher but how can she even get out the microscopes. 4F and microscopes! And they would enjoy, they should see the free-flow amoebae rolling along in a drop of ditch water, the paramoecia bumping about like ciliated Dodgems. It is all wrong. Sooze sees the chalk-strewn room, sees the still face of Mavis Kanji who waits stoically for the racket to subside so that Miss Powdrell can continue to teach her the Science she wishes to learn so that she can go to Training College and be a credit.

— Control is what she should be talking about, cries Sooze. Control! Not flaming Gowns!

— If we could just get rid of a few of the hell kids, says Margot. She tips the onion discards and spoon into the empty pottle, replaces the lid and holds the container in both hands.

Sooze agrees. — Jen Nation came at me with a chair yesterday, she says.

— Which is Jen Nation, asks Margot. Margot is five feet and slight.

— Huge! Punk. Sooze demonstrates Atlas without the world.

— Not Cissie Nation's sister?

— Maybe. Sooze shrugs. — Don't know.

Margot had a difficult interview last term with Mrs Nation who appeared at the door of the Clothing Room demanding satisfaction. She required to know why Margot picked on Cissie. If Cissie wanted to make pink taffeta dungarees she would make pink taffeta dungarees. Margot quite agreed. It was just that she thought the material mightn't . . . Margot

160

could get stuffed. Mrs Nation loomed over Margot who was eye to eye with the tan reindeers on the heavy blue jersey in front of her and told Margo where she could put herself and all fucken teachers. Who paid them anyway. Who did they think they were picking on kids like Cissie. And she knew where Margot lived, she added over her shoulder as she departed tip tipping across the courtyard in her high heels and white hailstone-spotted tights.

— Alec Tysler kicks open the staff room door. His arms are full of Art which he dumps on the table. — Sodding girls, he mutters.

— Go to Boys' High, says Carmen turning from her study of the cyclamen.

— I don't like knives, says Alec.

— We have the odd knife here says Sooze.

They continue their sagas of in-school experiences. Survivors, they draw comfort from escapes, near misses. Carmen reties the cord at the end of her plait. Any moment soon, she thinks, we'll be talking about the one that didn't go off.

— Why did they appoint a wimp to a tough school like this, asks Margot.

Alex is about to ask her if she really thinks *this* is a tough school, but refrains when he sees from the look of polite interest on Carmen's face that she is waiting for this remark.

— She's not a wimp, says Carmen. — Franklin never gives her a chance.

— She shouldn't need a *chance*, says Sooze. On and on and round and round in endless grinding circles the subject is discussed. The bell rings. Margot tosses her pottle in the Non Biodegradable where it lies on the plastic liner beside Jenni Murphy's bean sprouts which have gone off after all. This is the story so far.

4F have suffered Sooze's carefully prepared lesson on the Carbon Cycle with comparative calm. Sooze likes the Carbon Cycle. It explains a lot. All living things, she tells 4F, are born, grow, reproduce, die, then are buried if they are lucky. They rot and fertilise new growth. Life, explains Sooze, goes round and round in circles, but no one smiles. When the bell goes Sooze shoots the Vistavision screen up behind the blackboard, unplugs the slide projector, stacks away the slide carousel and heaves the heavy case off the table.

— Open the door please, she mutters to Jan who shrugs pained shoulders but obliges. Sooze heads off along the shining corridor trailing a cord which has slipped. She is surprised to see Mavis Kanji coming out of the girls' toilet. She dumps the projector case on the vinyl. — Mavis, she calls. Mavis moves hesitantly towards her. Sooze, Mavis, and the projector case form an island buffeted by waves of yelling females.

— Why weren't you in Science, Mavis? asks Sooze.

Mavis bursts into tears. Oh God, thinks Sooze, placing one leg firmly each side of the projector. Why did she ask. Her free period is a melting treat. She heaves up the projector case from the floor. — Come over here, she says. They move into an alcove, a backwater designed for such sanctuary, and sit on the mock leather bench. — What is the matter Mavis? asks Sooze. Mavis's tears flow from a deep well of sorrow. Her brown eyes are awash. They drip. Eventually, Sooze slots the pieces of the story together. Mavis wished to give Miss Powdrell some Basmati rice. — Basmati rice is the best rice in the world. Basmati rice is long, fine best tasting. Sooze nods. She knows about Basmati rice. — For you, gulps Mavis. — Well thanks Mavis, says Sooze, who bought some Basmati rice last week at the Indian dairy who have it occasionally. — I asked my mother, continues Mavis, but she said no so I took some. And then, and then . . . The memory is painful, the tears gush. — The big kids grabbed it from me like *this*, says Mavis snatching air with long narrow fingers, and poured it down the toilet. It is not funny Sooze tells herself but she knows Bryce will love it. — You shouldn't have taken your mother's rice Mavis, she bleats. — But it was for *you*,

Miss Powdrell! Sooze touches the heaving shoulder. — It was a very kind of you Mavis. It is the thought that counts says Sooze who is smug about clichés. — Don't worry about it any more. You must get back to class. Mavis's limpid eyes are wide. — But it is still *there* she says — Still sitting. I am trying to get it out!
— What!
— All through Science I am trying.
Mavis is in despair. She makes wooshing noises and wriggles a handle in the air. Her long hands are beautiful, the fingers skin and bone. — Oh God, thinks Sooze again. — Show me, she says. Together they move to the nearby toilets where paper lies deep on the floor and the graffiti is an open book.

Margot's Clothing period with 3G is going well. She teaches Home Economics which used to be called Home Science and is about to be called something else, but Margot teaches sewing and is happy to let it go at that. She demonstrates correct Cutting Out procedures. No hand is allowed to *touch* the giant scissors chained to the cutting table until Margot has checked Lay Out. Margot is meticulous, her small quick hands align, brush, straighten the length of printed denim on the table. — Always *check* girls, she says, that the pattern is printed straight on the material. However expensive the material . . . Margot does not finish the sentence. — Now the next thing is the darts. Margot likes third formers. Everyone likes third formers, or rather if they like any girls it is usually third formers or the occasional seventh former. 3G think Miss Maitland is neat which is a good description of Margot. She has the bobbing compactness of a scaup duck. She bounces back. All the girls are impressed by what Margot knows. They watch her. She knew when to stop wearing heavy belts slung low on her hips. She knew when to discard the ties which knotted, the boots which clanked. Last week she turned her bright pink collar down at the back and buttoned the shirt to the neck like the lead singer in Pet Shop Boys. She is thinking about removing her shoulder pads. The girls don't miss a trick. Margot's lover wears jandals both summer and winter. He is used to them he says, and so what.

Carmen has also had a satisfactory third period during which 5G played intelligent fast exhilarating netball. Carmen discussed strategy which is all important. She cannot understand why the fire of fifth form netball is so hard to maintain in the sixth and seventh forms. She would really like to know. Carmen is everywhere at netball. She leaps, blows her whistle, exhorts, seizes the ball in mid flight to demonstrate how Ema's shooting stance could be improved. — See! begs Carmen and Ema nods. The slack kids hide during Phys Ed and Carmen is damned if she is going to flush them out. Perhaps this is why Carmen is less impressed than Margot or Sooze with Miss Franklin's control.

Miss Franklin teaches French which makes it even more amazing. She has the French stream of 4F this period. Sooze is still head down over the girl's toilet with Mavis weeping by her side. 4F is by no means silent but Miss Franklin is in control. When she tells Jeanine to stop talking Jeanine stops talking. When Jess answers a question in English Miss Franklin says — *En francais s'il vous plait,* and Jess stumbles into Francais. Miss Franklin's bright hair is a banner, her eyes are a beacon as she leads 4F. She will teach 4F and they will learn. One or two will share her love for what she insists is the most beautiful language in the world. Miss Franklin and 4F have had serious discussions about the *Rainbow Warrior* and the French. Francais survives. It would break Sooze's heart. Miss Franklin tells 4F. — When I was in Paris as a postgraduate student (no desk lid bangs, no one moans), we were each asked for *un histoire* to explain why we were so angry. — In French? Miss Franklin is pleased. — In French, Bonnie. I explained to *le professeur* that I had received mail from New Zealand that morning and

could be angry with no one. — And then what asks Gee.
Miss Franklin tells them *en francais* and 4F get out their *cahiers*
like lambs.

Miss Tamp sits in her office with the sun on her back.
She studies a large chart of next year's timetable and wishes
once again that she could manage without part-timers who
make things so much more complicated. Miss Tamp's skill
with timetables is legendary. She has the vision of a three
dimensional noughts and crosses champion. She can *see* 4F
at Science in the lower lab there, 5B at Social Studies here.
The slight problem of the clash between Scholarship French
and Scholarship Applied Maths leaps to her gaze. She finds
the computer invaluable but likes to do her preliminary
shuffling with felt pens and cardboard. It is a tough round
but she is winning. Miss Tamp is very concerned about
the situation *vis a vis* Miss Franklin. Last night was impossible.
However she will worry about that later. At the moment
Miss Tamp is in her element. She turns to the keyboard.

Mrs Sinclair in the outer office has snatched a moment
to look at the Community College Winter Term Programme.
She moves the vase filled with Iris stylosa which she brought
from home, and spreads out the paper. She normally does
something each Winter. She can choose between Patchwork
and Patchwork for Christmas. Between Vegetarian Cooking,
Chinese Cooking, Microwave Cooking or Cake Decorating.
She can Keep Fit. She can try Living with Teenagers.
Dressmaking for Reproduction intrigues her until she sees
Porcelain Dolls on the next line. If she joins she must bring
her doll on the first night. Assertiveness for Women. Stress
Management. Mrs Sinclair sighs. She folds the paper and
puts it in her bottom drawer. The hell with it. But she
usually does something. She will show the newspaper to
Una Benchley.

But Mrs Benchley does not want to be pinned down. She
is quite dismissive when she comes into the staff room from

Gate Duty in the southerly. — Oh Thea! she says. — Not now for heaven's sake. She flops into an easy chair and stratches about in her bag labelled *Loot*. She finds a plastic bag, unwraps the Gladwrap and munches her vegemite, lettuce and wholemeal, staring straight ahead as though stoned. Mrs Sinclair is left with the page hanging. She folds it. Each class is one and a half hours long she reads but she knows this already. Beauty Unisex Complex catches her eye. This is an advertisement for Swift Scissors Hair Salon. There are Winter Specials.

Carmen, Margot and Sooze sit at the large table where the younger members of the staff congregate. There is no hierarchical seating structure in the staff room. It is just how things happen. Carmen is surprised when Miss Franklin, who usually occupies the third easy chair from the door, joins them, until she realises that the only vacant easy chair is beside Mrs Benchley. Carmen, who is convent-educated, moves a pile of books to accommodate Miss Franklin and offers her a chair. Miss Franklin thanks Carmen and gives her the smile of the ex-protagonist. Miss Franklin eats her Mealmates and apple. Carmen and Sooze, lean as Masai warriors, demolish greasies from the takeaway at the gate. Their precise polished fingers dip and pick. They lick their lips, suck their fingers, then scrub them with the scrappy paper napkins provided. Later they will wash. Margot, who wishes she had not eaten all her pasta salad at break, accepts some chips.

— How long have you been teaching, Miss Franklin? asks Carmen.

Miss Franklin peels her apple with spiralling expertise. — Thirty years, she replies.

There is silence as this remark is processed. It will take longer than the greasies. Thirty years thinks Sooze. Jeeze. Poor old cow thinks Carmen.

— Why have you stayed so long? says Margot, leaning forward to select a well done chip. She hates the pallid floppy ones. — Teaching I mean.

Miss Franklin knows their thoughts. Her brown eyes snap with pleasure. Her air is triumphant. — Because, she says, it amuses me to combat ignorance. And suck on that one thinks Carmen. There is no reply to Miss Franklin's statement. It sinks, rocking slightly from side to side like a coin subsiding in a mountain spring.

Alec Tysler lies back flattened in an easy chair. His outstretched legs impede progress to the coffee machine. There is some extravagantly high stepping. He stares at Carmen over the top of the *Dominion*. His eyes never leave her. He is ridiculous.

Carmen and Sooze go and wash. Margot makes do with a good scrub of tissues as she has not touched the chicken. The bell rings. The story continues.

Miss Tamp has put the timetable to bed, or rather to rest. There is only so much she can do at this stage. She sits very still at her desk gazing at one of the chimneys of the Old Block. The pot is the old-fashioned type, the smoke can go both ways. Miss Tamp thinks about Miss Franklin. Instinctively she reaches for her silver ballpoint and rough pad but they cannot help. What would she write. Friend of previous Head now dead. Wanted position herself. The cliché has been observed before and needs no clarification. There is no point in noting, Excellent teacher. Miss Tamp fingers the pencil. Destructive. Irrational. Impossible. Miss Tamp has tried everything. She has made allowances. She will not put up with it another minute. She is in the right and thus armoured. There will be no repeat of last night. Quick resolute thoughts shoot along Miss Tamp's nerve fibres. They leap the synapses. They stiffen the sinews. Miss Tamp reaches for the telephone. — Mrs Sinclair, she says — would you please get a message to Miss Franklin. Thank you. Ask her to come to my office, please, before she leaves school today. Yes. Thank you.

Miss Tamp leans back and twists Mother's garnet round and round her finger.

Miss Tamp's next concern is Fire Drill. She has decided, rightly, that advertised fire drills are not treated seriously enough. A slackness has crept in, not only, she fears, among the girls who linger and hide in the toilets. Midway though the last period Miss Tamp intends sounding the fire alarm. She has advised the Fire Service but not the staff. She looks at her Seiko and pushes her chair back. Miss Tamp leaves her office. She winks at Mrs Sinclair. They are conspirators.

The fire alarm shrieks through the school. Miss Tamp's heart is beating rather fast. She has always wanted to do that.

Sooze's wedge-cut hair swings back from her face as she lifts her head. Shit. Electrolysis of water is working perfectly. (Sooze is always grateful, surprised even, when her experiments work.) Oxygen is bubbling into one gas cylinder, twice the quantity of hydrogen is evident in the opposite cylinder. 3A are impressed. This is the real thing. I must have missed the warning spiel thinks Sooze who tends to think things are her fault. — O.K. girls. Sorry but we'll have to leave it she says, turning off the current. — Aw shit says Meryl. — Come along girls, leave your books. — They'll be nicked. — Leave your *books*. And hurry.

Margot is glad of the fresh air. Anything to get away from the combination of whooping chatter plus the buzz of the heavy duty machines which the kids foul up endlessly then scream for her to fix. — Amy! How many times! Press this *thing*, unravel the cotton, it's because you've put the thread around *here* instead of *here* . . . But Amy is itching to get back to her jump suit and wishes Margot would shut up and get off the chair. — Aw I get it, she lies. — And next time, says Margot, *don't* . . . But Amy is motoring. The Clothing Room is overheated. 5C are into being happy with their own bodies. Deodorants are out. Stephanotis is overwhelmed. — In order girls. Turn off the machines. In

order. Margot checks, turns off the lights and shuts the door.
— Straight to your *Station.* This way Penny. In Earthquake
Drill Margot is instructed to tell the girls to hide under their
desks when the plaster starts falling from the ceiling.

Miss Tamp and Mrs Sinclair take their own warning
seriously. They turn off, they shut down, they hitch their
skirts high and climb out the window onto the long vertical
fire escape ladder which they treat with respect, each foot
groping with care for the rung below. They are joined by
Mrs Benchley as she appears backwards from the staff room
Fire Escape window. She has had to clamber over a misplaced
sofa. — I thought I'd better come even though it *is* my
free period she tells Miss Tamp's departing hands. — But
of *course*, Miss Tamp replies to the behind above the Hush
Puppies. — What? — Oh never mind. There is an
unexpectedly long drop to the ground from the last rung
of the ladder.

Alec Tysler shepherds 4K from the chaotic Art room, rounds
up the stragglers, takes them to their Assembly Station by
the Library, discovers it's another bloody fire drill and ditches
them. He storms off across the hockey field to the Sports
Pavilion for a smoke. His narrow jeaned legs slice the air
as he fulminates with himself. What does she think they
are! No male would play games with his staff like that. Treat
them like kids for Chrissake.
   Alec bumps open the door of the Sports Pavilion with
his shoulder. Carmen turns, two panda netballs in her arms.
Alec flops onto the nearest bench. — What are you doing
here, he asks.
   — I work here replies Carmen, stowing the balls into
a locker which she locks with a key dragged up on a cord
from around her neck.
   — There's a fire drill says Alec as if it mattered. Carmen
stares around her mote-filled empire.
   — This is my Station she says. — I'm First Aid.

She could heal the whole sodding world. Alec moves to her.

Miss Franklin also dismisses her class as soon as she discovers the fire alarm is not genuine. The seventh form fan out chattering from their premature release, then, programmed as pigeons, swing back to the classroom block for their books. Miss Franklin is ropeable. Ropeable. What sort of a woman. What sort of a woman would *do* that. Lack of trust. Negation. Miss Franklin strides along the concrete path beside the hockey field in her ribbed *strumphosen*. She ignores the sun which shines through the few remaining leaves of the plane trees. She seethes beneath her lambswool then remembers. Tamp wants to see her. Good. Tamp will do that. Miss Franklin's pace quickens. She will cut across the hockey field to the Administration Block. She is on business bent.

She passes the Sports Pavilion. Miss Franklin inspects noise on principle. She tries the door handle then kicks the door open. Alec lies on the floor in the foetal position writhing in pain. A shaft of light from the skylight illuminates him, specks of dust are trapped in its rays. Carmen is against the lockers. Her face is scarlet, she is breathless and shaking. — He tried to rape me! she cries. Alec groans negation. Miss Franklin looks at the figure on the floor. Alec, speechless with pain, rolls his back to her. — Come with me, Miss Franklin says to Carmen and they leave the Sports Pavilion.

And thus it is that Miss Tamp's interview with Miss Franklin is deferred. She has after all made notes, marshalled her resources. She is calm and very determined. She will deal once and for all with Miss Franklin whose behaviour is impossible. Things cannot and will not go on like this. Last night will not be repeated. Miss Franklin must shape up or ship out though Miss Tamp does not think in these terms. There is a knock on the door. — Come in calls Miss Tamp and in burst Miss Franklin and Ms Doyle whom Miss Tamp last saw in confrontation but who are now obviously united in their mission. Miss Tamp hears them out and of course agrees. This must be dealt with *now*. Where is Mr Tysler? asks Miss Tamp. — He was in the Sports Pavilion says Miss Franklin. — On the floor says Carmen. Miss Tamp picks up her bag. — He won't still be there snorts Miss Franklin. Miss Tamp sets off on principle. Her cubans click along the empty polished corridors and concrete paths till she reaches the still building. The door is open, the Sports Pavilion is empty, a dusty stowage area for shadows, a quiet warehouse.

There is no answer from Mr Tysler's home number when Miss Tamp tries from her office on her return. She will try from home.

Carmen is shaken, though not from danger averted. Carmen is fit, she has studied Self Defence and her kick was well directed, but something is wrong with her. She stands staring at the face in the staff cloakroom mirror after Miss Franklin has finally left her. She removes a couple of long black hairs from the handbasin in front of her and fills it with cold water which she slaps against her face. She tells herself again not to be such a bloody fool. She clenches her fists with rage as her eyes prick with tears. She could kill the shit. It was all quite heavy. She is glad that Miss Tamp gripped the situation with such speed. He's had it. Carmen has had men. Bad enough anytime, but straight after Barry . . . She scrubs her face again. Sooze and Margot will have gone long ago. Carmen collects her gear from the empty staff room, takes her orange helmet from her locker and heads for her Honda. She will go to the gym and call in on Sooze on the way home. Bryce won't be there yet . . . Her eyes sting. — Shut up. Shut *up*. Get to the gym. Get to the gym. Have a sauna for God's sake.

Sooze is defrosting the chicken which she forgot to take out last night. It sits solid as the rock of Gibraltar in a

171

bowl of warm pink water on the bench. Sooze turns in surprise when Carmen walks in the back door, then takes her in her arms as she sees her face, her hands dripping on the black and white vinyl squares.

Margot arrives a quarter of an hour later for her Kaffe Fassett pattern and the story is retold. Sooze produces a wine cask and three glasses and she and Margot are supportive and loving to Carmen who is angry because she can't stop crying. Carmen, Margot and Sooze sit at the formica table and talk about rape, they talk about men, they talk about the school, they talk about themselves, they talk about rape, they talk about themselves.

Bryce comes home. He runs up the back steps two at a time and flings open the kitchen door. He takes a step back. — Hi, he says.

Aunt is delighted with her cyclamen. — The buds are like baby umbrellas she tells Mrs Sinclair. Aunt puts it on top of the TV as they like the warmth. Mrs Sinclair kisses Aunt's soft floury cheek and goes home to her teenagers and her curry which is still holding out.

Mrs Benchley stands at her kitchen bench on one leg and inspects the other, hauling it up behind with one hand and peering at it over her shoulder. She has just discovered that she has laddered her Columbines which were new on this morning. Bloody fire drill.

Mrs Toon did have a tin after all but it doesn't matter. She picks up Caesar and cradles him in her arms to love him. Caesar writhes and twists away to drop four footed on the floor, then rubs his hearth rug beauty against Mrs Toon's legs to love her.

It is six o'clock. Miss Tamp has lit the gas in the Hutt and pulled her curtains which show sailing ships butting across seas of blue glazed chintz. Miss Tamp loves tall ships. She stands by the small sideboard which sits against the back wall of her living room. There is a wooden cupboard each side and glasses behind glass in the centre. Miss Tamp bends for the square-shouldered bottle from the left hand side. She pours herself a gin, replaces the bottle and closes the door. The tonic is beneath a fizz saving cap in the Kelvinator. The kitchen is galley-shaped; not by Miss Tamp's design, it was like that when she bought the house, but it pleases her and works well. — It works, she tells visitors who admire its compact shape, its crisp white formica and navy blue cupboards. She adds a slice of lemon which makes all the difference to her gin and tonic. Miss Tamp has a business-like affection for her one gin each evening. She regards it as a friend. She likes advertisements on hoardings of foot square ice cubes and liquids which swirl in six foot glasses. Good old gin, she thinks as she moves to the sofa and adjusts its many cushions around her. Her choice in cushions is eclectic; there are cushions made from scraps of Persian rugs, dark velvet cushions for comfort, a Victorian embroidered patchwork one which cost the earth years ago in Camden Passage but she is glad she bought it. Miss Tamp settles for the News and sips. Bubbles gather round a lemon pip and carry it up to the surface, its ascension as effortless as a soul escorted to heaven by angels. The bubbles burst at the surface, the pip sinks, the bubbles rush to its aid and the process is repeated. Miss Tamp is pleased. She was Science originally.

Her small pleasure is punctured as she remembers that she has not yet spoken to Mr Tysler. She remembers the extraordinary dream she had last night about Mr Tysler or rather about the back of his neck. She had a vivid glimpse of the tough wrinkled skin in which was imbedded a tiny blue iridescent gastropod shell. Flesh had grown up around it so that only half the base below the pointed tip was visible. Miss Tamp is not Freudian about dreams but she does find them interesting and inexplicable. She must ring the man immediately. Miss Tamp knows that the more difficult something is the more quickly she must deal with it. She does not have to move. She reaches for her stiff leather bag, finds her Collins diary, checks under Staff and dials from the telephone by the sofa. No reply, she will have to keep trying. Damn. And she must ring Carmen to see how she is. No reply. Miss Tamp takes another sip of gin and sighs. And Miss Franklin. She will make another apointment with Miss Franklin tomorrow. Miss Tamp reaches for the tapestry footstool which repeats the nautical motif and heaves her legs onto it. She will never surrender.

Miss Franklin stands in front of a small oak table in her flat in Brooklyn. She enjoys the view though parking is a problem. In the centre of the table on which she has dumped 4F's marking is a brass tray with a sherry decanter and five glasses. Miss Franklin does not know what happened to the sixth glass as they had been in Jean's family for many years. The glasses are small hand-blown flutes. The decanter and each individual glass rest within a filigree silver holder. Also on the table is a photograph of Jean on the Milford Track laughing at a scavenging weka. Miss Franklin pours herself a Flor Fino from the decanter.

Jean died almost two years ago. Miss Franklin does not remember her as well as she used to. Or rather — she remembers everything she did and said. Every word of Jean's wisdom and ribald wit lives on, but sometimes Miss Franklin is surprised to discover how many hours can go by without a thought of her friend. She did not think this would happen. When Jean first died even making a cup of tea was a memorial. Miss Franklin remembers Jean, bright and sparky as chips, when she is in confrontation with the Headmistress whom Jean never knew. Miss Tamp is beneath contempt. But not quite. Each evening Miss Franklin tells Jean of every twist, every turn, every triumph in her continuing struggle with her friend's successor. She thinks of the scene in the Sports Pavilion. Of Carmen. She lifts her glass.

There is no end to this story.

Fast Post

— I've been thinking a lot about death, says my friend Sooze holding out her glass for more wine.

— Death, says her lover Bryce not wanting to commit himself.

— Why death, I say though of course I know. It's the sort of thing Sooze does.

My lover Cam doesn't say anything. He regards death as unacceptable for thought or talk. Cam is not interested in abstracts. His back is bent, his elbows just beyond his knees, his hands hang dejected as he stares at the floor.

We are at Sooze and Bryce's bach. Her parents' really, but Sooze and Bryce live there because their last flat folded and they can't find anything because they have no money so they can't find anything. Cam tells me they don't try. I can't comment on that but it's nice for us. We pile into the Skoda after work on Fridays and slip out to the coast in the slow lane. We take food and wine and we lie about and talk and drink a bit. Maybe go for a walk. We read a lot. There aren't many people you can read with. Most people say — Yes great, and you drag out your paperbacks and start. Then they tell you bits from their books. — Listen to this, they say then they read it and you have to listen perforce. Or else they read for a bit then lie on their backs and say — Aaah, and you know they're bored and want

175

to do something else and will suggest it soon, so you keep your head down and try and read your Barthelme faster which is unsettling because you can't do that.

It's not like that with Sooze and Bryce. We just read. Their son Jared who is measured in months not years lies around with us though of course we keep him in play. We more or less take it in turns. When it's Sooze's turn she props Jared up surrounded by cushions and holds one of his pudgy hands while she reads and kisses a dimple at the bottom of a finger occasionally to fool him. He doesn't mind.

— Death, says Sooze again staring at the sea.

— What about it, I say.

— Well what do you think about it, says Sooze. She wears a large sweater with a design loosely based on aboriginal rock carvings. The zigzag lines which go up are green, the zigzag lines which go down are orange, the small stick figures are red and the background is black. The aboriginal paintings I like best are the x-ray ones which show what the animal has eaten *in situ*.

— Or don't you, she says.

— Of course I do, I say. — What do you think I am.

— I don't, says Cam.

Sooze is incensed. — Why not.

— What's the point, says Cam.

— There's no point, says Sooze. — Except that it's inevitable.

— Right, says Cam so don't think about it.

— So doesn't it *interest* you?

People like Sooze think people like Cam are not as intelligent as they are. People like Cam don't care which would really surprise people like Sooze if they could believe it, but they never would so by and large it works out all right. People like Cam know about the shifting mud which can bury abstract thought and often does.

Enough, Cam thinks, is enough, and reality will be more than.

Bryce has made his decision. He puts out one finger and

176

corkscrews a piece of Sooze's hair around it which doesn't work as it's straight. He picks up her hand.

— Why hon he says. It's inevitable. No problem.

— What interests me I say, is why doesn't it worry us, I mean.

— It worries me says Sooze removing her hand.

Bryce really wants to know. He snatches both her hands across the table as though he's going to drag her into a square dance. — Why! he says.

— I mean when you think, I say quickly, that for thousands of years the best minds all over the world have fussed about life after death . . .

— And if you were a best mind and didn't you were burnt, interrupts Bryce.

— . . . so why don't *we* care, I say.

— I do says Sooze.

— But you're a scientist! says Bryce.

— Ha ha says Sooze who teaches it. — Oh it's not *that* she says. — I don't mind about death of the *body*.

— 'Change and decay, in all around I see', roars Cam who was a choirboy.

— What worries me is the *spirit*. The human consciousness continues Sooze. — Where does that go?

There is a pause. Cam inspects his jandals. Abstract thought has the same effect on him as pornography. He doesn't see the point and it's depressing. Cam is a builder. He wears short shorts at work, the front of which are hidden by a leather apron so heavy it looks like a costume prop for a medieval film. In it he keeps the tools of his trade to hand. — We're getting there he says, dropping onto his heels from a great height to hammer the floor. I still feel glad when I see him swinging up the street.

— It doesn't go anywhere hon says Bryce. — You've got to accept that.

— I can't says Sooze.

— That's why people invented religions I say. — Because they couldn't accept the death of the spirit, see.

— Well nor can I says Sooze getting up to go and check on Jared.

The sun is sinking but no one gives it a thought. Bryce tops our glasses then reaches up and scratches about with one hand in a top cupboard. — We had some corn chips somewhere he says coming back empty-handed.

Sooze also comes back and flops onto her chair. She puts both hands up and combs the fingers back through her hair. It looks better; the trapped air fluffs it up for a bit though the result was unintentional.

— O.K? I ask.

Sooze puts her hands together and lays a sleeping head on them. — O.K. she says.

I change the subject. — How're things going in the flat world I ask.

Bryce leans back tipping his chair, maintaining balance with one hand. Suddenly he is behind a large table top with desk furniture, a rock-a-bye blotter, an embossed leather folder, a paper knife. — We've been approached to house sit a place in Khandallah, he lets slip.

— Great I say. — I like 'approached'.

— Sounds as though they're on their knees says Cam. He removes a speck from his beer with his smallest finger.

Sooze smiles. She knows about Bryce but it's O.K.

— Yes she says. — Aunty Gret was on the lookout.

We know Aunty Gret. She paints. She gives us muddy water colours called Zinnias or Dahlias at Christmas and is a good sort and gets on with it.

— We haven't seen it and all that. I mean they haven't seen us and then there's Jared.

— Jared's flat on his back says Cam. — What can he do tenant-wise?

Sooze smiles. — Some people. Kids. You know, she says.

— Some people. Houses. You know, he says.

She puts out a finger and circles the vaccination mark on his bicep which dates from our overseas time. He flexes just for fun.

— What about Voltaire says Bryce untipping his chair.
Oh God.
Cam's bicep flops. — Who he says.
Sooze turns very slowly to stare at Bryce. — What about
him she says.
— Well he didn't get burned.
— Of course he didn't get burned snarls Sooze. — He
was too late wasn't he. For burning.
— He was exiled though wasn't he I say.
That's the trouble. We don't know anything. Just snatches.
— Have you got an Oxford Companion I ask.
Bryce yawns. — Not here.
— Pears?
He shakes his head.
— Voltaire said that if God didn't exist it would be
necessary to invent him I tell Cam, as though the man is
a new pleat for third form clothing instruction which I teach.
Cam likes it. — Good thinking, he says.
But Bryce won't let it go. — What did *he* think happened
to the human spirit after death he says.
Cam bends down to pick up Jared's plastic rattle from
his feet, examines it carefully, shakes it a couple of times
and places it on the table out of harm's way although there
is no harm.
— I reckon this Fast Post is a rip off he says.
And then we are fighting about Fast Post. Bryce says
it's essential. He has a letter from Levin ordinary post which
took five days. He slams the table, the rattle rolls onto the
floor. — Five days he says. — From *Levin*. Give me Fast
Post!
— That's what they want you to do. Cam is very angry.
His mouth tightens, the skin around his lips is white. When
he is eighty he will have deep lines, not fine bird track
wrinkles like some old men. — Pay twice as much. It's a
con!
I don't post much and I know nothing about it but that
doesn't stop me. — We should boycott it! I cry.

179

Bryce wants to hit me. All of a sudden we are hating each other, snarling and snapping at each others heels, circling around the ethics of Fast Post.

Sooze is not interested in Fast Post. She has taken the lasagne from the fridge and put it in the oven. She has prepared the salad but has not yet tossed it. She has chopped the chervil we brought and removed the Bleu de Bresse from the top of the fridge where it has been ripening. Sooze presses it between the slats of its small wooden cage. She seems pretty happy with its condition as she releases and unwraps it. She rinses her hands and shoves her hair back before curling up on the divan to clutch a calico patchwork cushion she made years ago. The design is called Cathedral Windows, not easy.

— What I do believe she says over the cushion top, is that two thousand years ago a really good man lived and died and if we could all live according to his commandments . . .

Bryce has had enough. He is on his feet, a tormented big cat loping the few steps from door to table, swinging in rage to confront her. — God in heaven! he shouts. — What's got into you!

— I can't stop thinking about death, Sooze mumbles into the cushion. Cam is determined to help. He leaps up from the table and sits beside her, pulling the cushion from her face.

— Look Sooze he says. — There's nothing to it. Don't worry about it. He takes her hand. — I promise he says smiling. — I nearly snuffed it. Didn't I Margot. In Milan.

— Yes I say.

— All you feel is surprised. You know, like it's not happening. Death, Cam insists, is for other people and when it's you you're surprised. That's why they'll never stop the road toll. — Disbelief, he says. — That's all I promise.

Milan is a challenge. It doesn't lie back and welcome you like Venice say. You have to track it down, find the good bits, work on it. We headed off from the station with our packs.

It was one of those hotels which always surprise me by not starting on the ground. It was on the third floor, recommended by *Let's Go*. Ground floor was shops, first and second another hotel, and the Pensione Famiglia Steiner on the third. Space was used twice — coffee and rolls were served in last night's bar. The family, mother father and three dark-eyed bambinas watched TV at night lined up on straight chairs against the wall in the slit office space. You put down the lavatory seat in the tile-lined box and turned on the shower. In England where dirt cheap means it, it would have been filthy but it was clean, the cotton bedspread white white, the linoleum shiny, the paint scrubbed.

We had a coke in the bar when we arrived, dumping our packs in the space labelled Rucksack in six languages. I flopped down beside a man at a table while Cam moved to the self-service dispenser. The guy had one of those street-wise faces, blunt features, pointed ears set at the slope, quick eyes. His haircut and fingers were short and stubby, the rest of him long and lean and pretty to watch. Cam was having trouble with the machine. The guy was up, instant and agile as a gibbon. He demonstrated the thing to Cam who thanked him. — That's O.K. the man said.

He came from Manchester, a male model. Milan was the place, even though the agents took half your fee in commission. Milan is the world centre of male fashion he told us glancing at Cam's jandals. Milan is the big time where it's at. He'd been there three weeks and was doing O.K. so far though the whole thing was a real hassle. You've got to sell yourself he told us. No one else will.

— Yeah said Cam. — Nice guy he said as we went to our room.

We flaked out on the bed and slept. They don't let you sleep on second-class Eurail. The bastards wake you all the time.

Cam came to first. Making love all over Europe is different each time; well surroundings, externals. The late afternoon sun fell through the net curtains. Cam's legs were pure gold. — Tea? he asked afterwards, lifting my foot to kiss a toe. — Mmm I said, easy either way but why not. He hauled himself off the bed and assembled our survival equipment, our artifacts. A narrow little Cretan saucepan from the market in Heraklion, an immersion heater, adaptor plugs. Lying on my back I heard the familiar clanks and knocks of illicit tea making.

— Haven't met one like this before he said.

— Nnn? I said watching the patterns of light caught in the net.

The flash was followed instantly by Cam's naked body hitting the floor. He lay stiff, catatonic, every muscle locked. The plug was smoking, the air acrid. I was on my feet leaping to fall on him. I yanked his head back chin to ceiling and cupped my mouth over his mouth and nose and breathed in, out, in, out. At first I was shaking so hard I couldn't breathe deeply but the rhythm took over. Breathe, look, breathe, look. It didn't take long, half a minute or an hour. Cam. Don't stop. Breathe, stop, look, breathe, stop, look. His chest moved slightly, stopped, then gradually rose and fell in beautiful repetitive movement. My breasts stroked him, his eyes opened. — Nice he said. I dragged him onto the bed and shook for an hour as I lay beside him, watching, holding him, being held.

He wouldn't tell the owner. — He'd kick us out. It wasn't the plug. My fault, no mucking furries.

Next morning we sat drinking coffee and holding hands, you can do it. The amiable hairy proprietor heated the rolls in a mini oven beside the coke dispenser. Last night's bar was dark brown, benches, walls, an old sofa. The air had been there for some time. The male model sat reading a torn copy of the *Daily Mirror*. Jerry his name was.

The most beautiful girl I have ever seen dumped an enormous pack in the space by the door and subsided at the other table. She was six feet at least and walked haughty, slender, breasts firm beneath a Benetton T-shirt, her hair a stream of silver down her back. — Hi said Jerry. She said nothing, but dipped her crisp profile in recognition. German she must be, German, an ice maiden from a schloss in the pines. Or Swedish, saunas and birch twigs. Cam's hand moved in mine. His eyes were feeding on her. We all were. Beautiful women slay me.

She ordered coffee from the owner who seemed calmer than the rest of us. She drank it staring straight ahead then replaced the white cup with precision, centering it with care on its unmatching saucer. She lit a cigarette. I let Cam's hand go. Jerry was trying not to look at her, riffling the tattered *Daily Mirror*, flinging it onto the floor, snatching another from the pile on the end of the sofa. He was a cartoon figure, an expectant father from the days when fathers sat in waiting rooms with discarded papers at their feet.

She ground out her cigarette, stood up and shouldered her huge pack with one dip and lift. Jerry was on his feet. — You're not going! he cried. — Now!

She nodded and walked out, heading towards the cage lift. Jerry leapt after her, they disappeared. The owner picked up her cup, flicked the table with a checked duster and headed for his operations centre.

— Jeeze, whispered Cam.

— So *beautiful* I gasped. What was their relationship? One night? Ten years? Nothing?

Cam shook his head. The square brown room smelt very used. We were in shock, bereft, sitting there staring at the space she had filled.

— So you see, says Cam now squatting on his heels, staring up into Sooze's face for added conviction. — It's nothing.

183

Sooze shakes her head in the slightest possible rejection but she is grateful and smiles to tell him so, her hand on his knee.

— It's not that Cambo, she says. She sits up busily and knuckles a finger against her nose. — Did you see Mantegna's *Dead Christ*, she asks.

— We tried says Cam who likes looking at paintings.
— The place was shut. Marg got the time wrong.

I kick his behind which unbalances him into Sooze's lap. One of our failures.

— It's the foreshortening. Sooze moves her head in slower wonder. — Amazing, she says.

Bryce has been reading the *Evening Post*. He folds it and slaps it on the divan as he stands to refill the glasses.

— In the morgue, he says, stretching his arms way above his head then letting them flop, they tie your name on your big toe. The right one. For identification.

Sooze Cam and I stare at him in silence, then turn to the dark sea, listen to it roll.

— I'd hate to be buried says Cam.

184